CW01082231

CLAIMED HARDER

By

Em Brown

CLAIMED HARDER

CHAPTER ONE

DARREN
Present

*C*oming inside of Bridget felt *intense*—so intense, I didn't actually enjoy it all that much. Her ass felt amazing, but my climax was akin to slamming my fist into a brick wall. Feels good to let out all that steam, not so good on the knuckles.

Withdrawing from her, I stumble back and collect my senses. Wiping off my cock, I pull up my pants and survey her, her wrists still tied to the exposed pipes of the basement we're in, her dress bunched up about her hips, her panties wrapped below her ass, my cum dripping down her thighs.

The nice thing, the loving thing, to do is untie her, wrap my arms about her, the way I used to after we'd had sex, hold her and see to her aftercare if we had an intense play session.

But that was before she left me.

It took me over two years to track her down.

Partly because I had wasted time barking up the wrong tree. I thought maybe she had gotten together again with her ex-boyfriend, Dante. And maybe she had, though he swore they hadn't seen each other in years, but it took a little while to convince me that they were no longer together. After exhausting Amy's family, the two other women Bridget had shared an apartment with, instructors, and classmates at Cal, came the arduous task of tracking down a woman named Coretta.

You did a good job making it hard for me to find you, I compliment Bridget as I eye her rump, still flush from the spanking I gave her with my wet shirt. That delicious ass has been on the receiving end of many different implements: the paddle, a tawse, the flogger, and even a bouquet of nettles. I want the chance to apply all those things to her backside again.

But does she want it?

She did come on my cock, but that doesn't mean she wants to be with me.

Turning her to face me, I grab her jaw, which pushes up her cheeks. "You came without permission, Bridge."

"I'm—I'm sorry," she stutters.

"You know better than that."

She lowers her lashes. I hate that she still looks attractive to me, especially with her cheeks flushed from having just come.

"What's the matter?" I ask. "You out of practice?"

She looks at me with emotions too mixed for me to figure out. "Yes. I—I haven't been with anyone..."

I snort. "You expect me to believe you?"

Glancing down briefly, she doesn't object right away. That upsets me.

I reach between her legs. "Who'd you give my pussy to?"

Her lashes flutter as I stroke her flesh.

"Who'd you get wet for?" I ask.

She moans before answering, "No one."

"No one? What about Dante?"

She looks distressed.

"Thought so," I say with anger as I rub her clitoris.

A few minutes later, she starts to whimper and squirm. Withdrawing my fingers, I place them in her mouth. She knows to suck my digits clean. My cock stiffens at the suction upon my fingers.

But first, there's the matter of her punishment.

I tear off her panties, a flimsy and somewhat old pair. I bought her nice underwear when she was with me, but she doesn't want to have anything to do with me. Opening her mouth, I shove the panties between her lips. Stepping away, I look around and see cords of rope hanging on one wall. I pick a monofilament polypropylene rope. My favorite is jute, but this will still work well. After unwinding the rope, I tie a knot into it. I wrap the rope about her hips and between her legs, securing the knot right at her clit. Taking another cord of rope, I bend one of her legs, bind her ankle to the top of the thigh, and slip the rope under her knee before tossing it over a pipe overhead. With one leg hoisted in the air, she wobbles on her standing leg. The high heels she has on don't help.

Good.

Grabbing my wet shirt, I look at her one last time before heading out and closing the basement door behind me.

CHAPTER TWO

BRIDGET
Past

*T*he door swings open, slamming against the wall, leaving a dent where the doorknob hit it.

"Amy!" Simone admonishes my roommate from where she and I sit at the table having leftover pizza for breakfast.

"You won't believe this!" Amy squeals.

"I'll put door stop on our shopping list," I tell Simone.

"You guys! You will not believe where I just got invited to next weekend!"

I have a feeling her invitation resembles the one I received from Darren last night. Part of me doesn't believe Darren was serious.

"The John Legend concert?" Simone guesses.

"He plays the following weekend," I tell her.

Amy hops up and down. "No, it's not John Legend. It's Thailand!"

"Like the country Thailand?" Simone asks.

"Yesssss!" Amy hops in circles now.

"Cool. When would you be going?"

"Next weekend. Luckily, my passport's in order since I went to France with my family last summer. But can you believe it? Thailand!"

"Is this with the JD Lee you've been talking about?"

"Of course!!" Amy's eyes widen with a realization. "I've got to go shopping!"

She grabs a slice from the open box of pizza between me and Simone before rushing off to our room.

Simone looks at me in some disbelief. "Thailand? Next weekend? That's short notice, but this guy must be serious about Amy. By the way, how did it go with *your* guy?"

My cheeks become warm. After Darren left, unable to focus on my paper, I went to see if Simone was up for watching *The Wire* and found she had fallen asleep. I channel flipped for a while, eventually dozing off on the sofa with CNN playing in the background.

"Good, I think," I respond. "I got invited to Thailand, too."

Simone's bottom lip dropped. "I am so missing out! Are you guys for real?"

"I don't know how serious Darren's invitation was."

"Darren is the cousin of Amy's guy?"

I nod and take a sip of my morning orange juice. Not the best beverage pairing with pizza.

"Damn," Simone sighs. "These guys must be loaded if their idea of a next date is Thailand! Is there another cousin I can date?"

"Julie okay with that?" I tease, referring to a woman whom Simone, who's bi, has been seeing.

"I think she'd understand if I get to jet off to Thailand at a moment's notice," Simone joked. "These guys must be serious about you and Amy."

I shake my head. "Just because they can afford to take someone to Thailand doesn't mean a thing."

I suddenly wonder what costs Darren expects me to cover. I certainly can't afford the plane ticket.

"I bet guys with money like to show off to anyone and everyone," I add. I think about the designer clothes Darren wears, the fancy nightclub he owns, and the Porsche Pana-whatever car he drives that he and I joked about as a penis extension.

Simone reaches for another slice of pizza topped with mushroom and pineapple. I had thought it an odd combination at first, but to my surprise, it works. "So you don't see it as serious?"

"Definitely not. We don't know each other that well. He's not even my type."

"What's your type?"

"Someone non-glamorous who wouldn't be caught dead at a fundraiser for Drumm."

"*You* were at one."

"I didn't know it was a fundraiser for him! Did I

tell you Darren's ex is dating Drumm's son, Eric?"

"She sounds like a bitch."

I reach for a second slice of pizza for myself. "She's not wrong when she says that Darren is 'slumming' it—"

"Bitch."

"—but I'm not his type in other ways, too. I'm opinionated, politically progressive, *not* a lingerie model..."

"Opposites attract all the time."

"But those attractions don't last, or they make for a rocky relationship."

"So the sex is good, then."

Recalling how Darren made me climax through a foot massage, I don't respond right away.

Simone grins. "Yeah, I knew it. It has to be something if all that you said is true."

"It's good," I mumble into a bite of pizza.

"Well, enjoy it. I bet Thailand is a great place to have sex."

"Even if Darren is serious about it, I can't go. I don't have a passport, I have classes—"

"Get the class notes from someone, and Amy can help you with stats."

"—and my job and my current internship."

"How long are you going to be gone?"

"I don't even know. Thailand seems so...so random. I thought Darren was joking."

"You're going to turn down an all-expenses-paid trip to Thailand?"

14

"I don't know that it's 'all-expenses-paid,'" I continue to protest.

"Well, if you're not going, I'll go in your place."

The conversation turns to a different topic after that. After we clear the table, I head back into the room I share with Amy, ready to attack the paper I was trying to work on yesterday before Darren showed up.

Amy's clothes cover the floor.

"Sorry," she says as she digs through a drawer. "I could have sworn I had brought my bikini back here from home, though a new one would be more fun. But the stores aren't likely to have a great selection of swimwear this time of year. I'm going to have to order something online, which isn't as fun as trying things on. Plus, I'm going to need a dress for the wedding."

"Wedding?" I ask as I perch on the bed and watch as Amy holds up a short-sleeve sweater in front of a mirror.

"JD's sister is getting married in Thailand."

So Thailand wasn't as random a destination as I'd thought.

Amy whirls around, her eyes bright with stars. "Can you believe how fast things are moving with JD? I mean, I'm going to be meeting his *family*."

"That's usually a significant step," I acknowledge with hesitation.

I still have questions about JD. I can't quite put my finger on why I have reservations. Maybe because he comes across so cool and smooth. Amy's falling hard for the guy, and I don't want her to get hurt.

To offer my way of looking at things, I share, "Darren actually invited me, too, but I doubt he considers us a serious relationship."

Amy stares at me agog. "What?"

"He came by yesterday. Asked if I wanted to go to Phuket."

"No way! He's got to be into you, Bridget! And to think, you threw soda in his face when you first met!"

I chuckle now, though the dominant feelings that night had been anger and hurt, followed by mortification, remorse and sheepishness. Darren had approached me and disparaged the sweater I was wearing at his swanky club. Apparently he had thought I was part of some prank being pulled on him, but I didn't know that. So, yeah, I threw my Coke at him for being so mean. I also didn't know at the time he was the club owner and JD Lee's cousin.

"How can he not consider you guys as serious if he's introducing you to his family?" Amy asks.

"Because we haven't even gone on an official date."

Amy waves a dismissive hand. "What makes a date 'official' anyway? Like it has to be over dinner at a restaurant or a movie? Honestly, I think that's old-fashioned. Did you guys have sex?"

I nod. It was unlike any sex I had ever had before. Since Simone was just across the hall in her room, I was worried that we'd make too much noise. Darren had covered my mouth and nose with his hand. I remember the panic of not being able to breathe. Somehow, it had led me to the most intense orgasm I had ever experienced.

"Did JD mention how long the trip's going to be?" I inquire.

"A week, maybe week and a half."

I balk. "That's a long trip."

"If you're going to fly all the way to Asian, you don't want to have to turn around a few days later."

"You're not worried about missing that much school?"

Amy stares at me like she can't believe I would even ask such a thing. "How often does one get invited to Thailand? Thailand!"

We both start at the sound of a chirping beep.

"What's that?" I ask.

"Oh, it's a monoxide detector," Amy says with a roll of her eyes. "My mom freaked out when she read in the newspaper that a family of four passed away in their sleep at a local motel because of a faulty heater or something, so she sent me one. It must be low on batteries. I should just plug it into the wall."

While she tries to find a free outlet, my cellphone buzzes with a text. It's from Darren, though I don't remember ever giving him my number.

> For your passport,
> send me your
> headshot. You can be
> smiling but no teeth
> can show.

Did I actually say I was going to go? As I replay my exchange with him, I don't recall saying definitively that I would go. I didn't say I wouldn't, but Darren has these instances where it seems he just expects me to do what he says. And I have because, so far, they've been minor things, like getting into his car after he's offered to drive me to the grocery store. But I'd better assert myself more before he thinks he'll always get his way.

I text back:

> We should talk more
> about this.

Seconds later, I get a text:

> Come over to the
> club tonight.

I debate spending another night with Darren when I still have my outline for my health policy paper to finish. I text Darren:

I'll let you know later
if I can make it.
Have a paper to work
on.

He responds:

Don't play hard to get.

A little miffed, I type back:

I'm not! I really do
have classwork. FYI,
I'm a college student.

He texts:

Then go get it done
instead of texting
me. I'll expect you at
ten o'clock.

I purse my lips, then text:

Anyone ever tell you
how bossy you are?

His answer:

You haven't seen the
half of it.

I blink several times. How is that supposed to attract me to go to Phuket with him? A childish part of me wants to tell him I'm not coming tonight, so he knows I'm not about to go over to his club just because he says so.

Instead, I write:

I'll update you later.

That leaves it open for me to decide to go or not. I'm about to put my phone down when I receive a final text:

No need. Just come
at ten.

Is he trying to annoy me on purpose? I wonder.

"Hey, you wanna go shopping with me?" Amy asks. "We can either hit up Union Square or go to a mall in the 'burbs."

"I should get to working on these grant applications for my internship," I reply. "Plus, I don't know that I'm going to Thailand."

Amy looks at me as if I've said something sacrilegious. "Why would you not?"

"Between classes, my job and internship, I don't

know that I can get away. Don't you have your first set of midterms in two weeks?"

"I'll tell my professor I had to go be with family. It's not that big a deal."

I haven't kept track of how many classes or shifts Amy has missed at the restaurant where she works, but her priorities seem to have shifted even though she usually stresses over her grades because she wants to make it into a med school like Stanford or Johns Hopkins. But maybe Amy will settle back to her old self once some of JD's luster starts to fade.

Getting off the bed, I sit at my desk and turn on my computer. Time to make headway on my paper. Truth is, I want to see Darren tonight.

CHAPTER THREE

DARREN
Past

"What are you smiling at?" asks JD as we work out in his home gym, which is equipped with several different pieces of cardio and weight equipment.

I put down my phone and pick up a pair of dumbbells to resume my biceps curls. "Giving Bridge a hard time."

With a barbell situated over his shoulder, JD does a set of squats. "Who?"

"Bridget Moore. Amy's roommate."

"You're kidding. You banging her?"

"We got together a couple of times."

JD stares at me. "Why?"

The truth is, I don't know. She's not really my type, but for some reason I'm drawn to her. Maybe there's some truth to what they say about pheromones. But I'm sure I'll get bored of her eventually.

"She good at giving head or something?" JD asks.

"Don't know. Haven't done that yet."

JD shakes his head. "What's up with you? Are you trying to get back at Kimberly?"

Kimberly is my most recent ex-girlfriend, now dating the son of a billionaire real estate developer turned governor of Florida and presidential hopeful.

I don't bother answering JD because getting back at an ex wasn't even something I would have considered doing as a teenager, let alone as a twenty-eight-year-old adult man.

"Just trying something different," I muse aloud. "I invited her to your sister's wedding."

JD practically drops the barbell, which weighs over a hundred with the weights. "You *what?*"

"Invited her to Phuket."

JD stares at me again, then shakes his head. "I hope she doesn't wear that ugly-ass sweater of hers to the wedding."

That "ugly-ass sweater" is what got me off on the wrong foot with Bridget. I thought she was working with Ron to pull a joke on me. After approaching her with that assumption, I wound up with Coke splashed in my face.

"I'll take care of that," I respond after I set the dumbbells back on the rack and move over to the bench press.

"I guess Amy will be happy her friend gets to tag

along."

Lying down, I settle myself below the barbell. "Things getting serious between you two?"

"Have you ever known me to be serious? I mean, Amy's as cute as they come, and she's got this tight little pussy, so she'll last a month or two longer than others. I don't have to contend with a mom like yours."

JD's mom ran out on his father when JD was five. He grew up close to his father, who's now retired from the *Jing San* Triad and lives in Sydney.

"My mom's more concerned with getting me out of triad business than seeing me settled," I say before I lift the barbell off the stand and lower it to my chest.

"That's why I'm glad I don't have a mom. Has anyone ever talked to her? I mean, I get that she doesn't want you to end up in jail like your dad, but the chances of that happening are slim. We took care of Stan. We sent a potent message."

Stanley had turned state's witness after getting arrested with several hundred kilos of cocaine on him, leading to my dad's conviction for counterfeiting. Though Stanley's body remains missing, photos of him naked—missing his fingers, toes, and penis—have circulated among triad members. His defense attorney has also gone missing.

"She doesn't want me dead," I say after doing a

set of twelve and setting the barbell back.

"That was a fluke. Being knifed by a racist inmate."

That's what I believe, though my mother wonders if my father had been killed so that he doesn't pull a Stanley Locke. I tend to think if that was the case, my father would have been killed a lot sooner, not two years into his sentence.

"Nothing's going to happen to you," JD continued. "You know, Hao Young really would like to see you follow in your dad's footsteps in counterfeiting."

I start on my next set. Lee Hao Young, a high-ranking Operations Officer in the *Jing San,* had approached me already.

"I don't think I'll take him up on that."

"'Cause you're trying to make your mom happy? Don't you want to continue your old man's name? Your dad's a legend."

"Death changes people," I grunt as I push the weights up.

"You afraid of death?"

I consider his question because I'm oddly not. I'd rather live, for sure, and it would suck for my mother if I died prematurely. My father often said that the man who doesn't fear death has the winning hand.

"No," I answer, "but there's nothing that appealing working ops for counterfeiting."

"Don't you want to climb the ranks? Where's

your ambition? You just want to run The Lotus for the rest of your life?"

I don't. In fact, I can't really see myself running it for more than two or three years more. Cheryl can manage the club just fine without me.

Done with squats, JD switches to cardio and gets on the rowing machine. "And what about your dad's legacy? You just gonna walk away from that?"

I think about what my father would have wanted me to do: continue his name in the triad. Like JD, who took over his father's job importing additives and adulterants used to cut cocaine.

Moving up in the *Jing San* is a logical step. The triad is my world, my family. I know I wouldn't want to work for anyone else, and it's not like I have any special talents to do anything else.

"I'll think about it," I tell JD.

"Good. It's an honor to be recruited by Lee Hao Young, you know."

JD recently expanded what he does after being approached by Hao Young a few months back. I don't know the details, and I haven't asked because the less I know, the better.

*****

Bridget sends me an update in the afternoon:

Got a lot done, so I
can come over

tonight with Amy.

Like you weren't ever going to, I think to myself. But if I text that back, Bridget might change her mind just to prove a point.

I recall the many times she had come at my place, and in that small bedroom in her apartment six blocks from campus. She's going to want more of that. The question floating in and out of my head is whether or not she'd go beyond vanilla sex.

As if reading my mind, while we're sitting in my usual spot on the second floor of The Lotus later that evening, JD asks, "You plan to show Bridget the other side of your club?"

The Lotus has two sections: one for the regular patrons, comprising a good chunk of triad members and their friends and associates, and the other for those who also engage in BDSM. I have distant relatives who play at a place like The Lair, which isn't bad, though the place tends to also get gawkers and newbies. Before The Lotus, I'd played a few times at a placed called The Cross, a unique club where gang members manage to mix without getting into fights with one other. But I like my own place. It's not as crowded as The Cross, and I control the clientele.

"Too early to tell," I say in response, imagining how Bridget would respond being tied to a St. Andrew's cross, my flogger whipping over her naked body. I haven't actually seen her completely naked yet. "Would you take Amy?" I ask JD.

JD pours himself a shot of *baijiu*. "Maybe. I don't know that I have enough patience."

That was a challenge for JD. He'd get aroused, want to come, and after he came, he wasn't all that interested in finishing the scene.

One of my servers comes up to refill the water glasses on the coffee table. She smiles at me in a coy manner while JD looks her over, his gaze resting on her ass as she bends over to pour the water.

"That's some tasty-looking putang," JD says after the server heads back down the stairs. "And I saw the look she gave you."

"If Cheryl catches her flirting with me, she'll be fired faster than you come," I reply. My manager is no-nonsense, and in a club like mine, a tight ship is needed.

"Ha, ha," JD replies sarcastically. He looks past me. "Speak of the devil."

Cheryl comes up to me and tells me that Manny wants to talk.

"He's not asking me to allow more Park Street Boyz into my club?" I inquire.

Manny recently partnered with Tim Tran of the PSB on opening massage parlors in the 'burbs. The PSB used to fight over turf with the *Jing San* in the old days, before the triad moved into higher-level crimes.

"He says it's personal," Cheryl replies. "He's

28

waiting in the office."

I check the time on my watch. It's just past ten. Bridget should be here soon. But I make my way down to the office.

"What's up?" I ask Manny, who's a little younger than me but looks older.

"You know how I'm working with Tran to get these massage parlors opened?"

I sit behind my desk and notice Manny doesn't sit down. He tends not to when he's anxious.

"That going okay?" I ask.

"Yeah, yeah, it's going really well. We've got locations and business permits for three of them already."

"That's fast."

"Well, I used our connect in the county business licensing department, and we made sure all our sites are in unincorporated areas. Now we just need to staff them up and get the word out."

"So what did you need to see me about?" I inquire, betting that it has something to do with money. Manny is better at spending than making it. Right now, he's dressed in a burgundy silk shirt and black Armani pants and jacket.

"I just need to chip in a little more investment to help make sure everything is up and running smoothly. Plus, I told Tran that I had a connect that could help supply the women."

"I can't help you there," I reply. Sex trafficking is my least favorite part of the triad business.

"Yeah, yeah, I can figure that piece out myself. Word is JD might be groomed for that."

I don't reply. Is that what JD's new project with Lee Hao Young involves?

"But if you could help with the capital end..." Manny continues.

"How much?"

"Just a couple thousand."

"Exactly how much?"

"Six or seven thousand."

"How is 'six or seven' just a 'couple thousand?'"

Manny chuckles nervously. "I hated math. But you can spare that, can't you?"

I narrow my eyes. "Have you tried selling your clothes?"

Manny rubs the back of his neck. "You'd be helping me out in a big way, Darren. Tran was really impressed when he was here. He'd like to come back. I can't look cheap now."

"Your idea to invite him here," I point out with little sympathy. This isn't the first time Manny has asked me for money.

"Think of it as an investment. I'll pay you back. With interest. How 'bout that?"

"Manny, you haven't paid me back the twenty bucks I lent you to buy cigarettes when we were sixteen."

"This is different. These massage parlors are going to make bank. More people have moved out of the city lately, so demand in the suburbs has skyrocketed."

"Massage parlors in the 'burbs aren't new."

"There's more demand than supply."

"What is the six or seven thousand going to buy?"

"One of the parlors is a little close to residential, so we might need to retain a lawyer in case neighbors want to take us to the planning commission or city council or some shit like that."

"What else?"

"Maybe more massage beds."

I stare hard at Manny. "And how much is going to your gambling debt?"

Manny chuckles nervously again. "You know me well, don't you, Darren?"

I don't say anything, which makes Manny fidget more.

"Those PSB boys play a mean game of poker," Manny says.

"How much?" I demand.

"Eighteen hundred. But like I said, I'll pay you back. With interest. If you loan me this money, man, I promise you'll make it back. Because once people like Lee Hao Young see how successful I am, they'll finally take me seriously. And, unlike JD, who basically inherited everything from his dad, I'll be self-made. And that's worth a hell of a lot more. Self-made."

"How do I know, if I give you any amount of money, that you aren't going to spend it on more

Armani suits?" I question.

"Darren, I've never been more serious about anything before."

Manny speaks in earnest, but this wouldn't be the first venture that excited him and that he was convinced would make him. Poor Manny has struck out more times than an entire baseball team.

I consider offering to pay expenses, like the lawyer, directly, but I don't want my name associated with the parlors. Plus, I don't want to deal with any administrative hassles of making individual payments.

I sigh and get up, ready to see if Bridget has arrived. "I'm not investing in any massage parlors, but I'll loan you eighteen hundred to cover your gambling debt. If I don't get any of that back in three months, that's the last dime you'll ever get out of me."

"Darren, you won't regret this!"

"I already do." I walk past him, pausing only to say, "No more Armani."

Outside the office, I inform Cheryl to handle the disbursement to Manny.

"Your guests, Amy and Bridget, arrived five or so minutes ago," my manager says. "They're up on your floor."

I head upstairs where I find Amy Liu, a petite young woman who's lightened her normally black hair, curled up next to JD, but no Bridget.

"She went to the restroom," Amy explains.

Luckily, JD and Amy are so into each other, I don't have to make a lot of small talk while I wait for Bridget. After more than ten minutes pass, I wonder aloud if Bridget's okay. Looking over the balcony, I don't see her anywhere.

"I'll go check on her," Amy offers.

JD turns to me. "So what did Manny want?"

"Money."

JD rolls his eyes. "What a fucking loser."

"Not everyone's born rich."

"Manny could have a billion dollars, he'd still be a fucking loser."

Like Drumm. But I keep the thought to myself. JD still wants me to join him as one of the ground-floor investors of the new golf and spa resort that Eric wants to build upstate.

"He's always been a hanger-on," JD says. "He's been tailing us around since we were kids, always that third wheel slowing us down. Remember that time we ditched him in West Oakland back in high school? He wet his pants. I swear, if his mom hadn't married a Vanguard, he'd be out of here in seconds."

"Manny just wants to be like you."

"I always thought he wanted to be like *you.* Either way, it's irritating as hell."

I recall what Manny said about JD's possible expansion into sex trafficking. Unlike Manny, JD respects my desire to know less rather than more.

Amy returns and tells me, "Bridget wasn't in the

restroom. I'm not sure where she is."

I look over the balcony again at the dance floor, the dining area, and the bar. No Bridget. I make my way to the third floor, which is a smaller seating area with a few highboys. No Bridget. Where could she have gone?

CHAPTER FOUR

BRIDGET
Present

I hate it when he ties me up in asymmetric suspension because I can't relax into the rope bondage as much. Balancing on one foot—when that foot is in chunky five-inch heels—is no fun. Plus, the sensation of being off-kilter is making it hard for me to think and plan my escape. Every time I wobble, I seem to feel the crotch rope even more against my clit, reminding me of the orgasm that I had come close to having when Darren was fondling me between the legs.

After all these years, after all that I've learned about him, my body still goes crazy for him. It's like my lust is Pavlov's dog. All Darren has to do is caress me, and I'm a wet, hot mess. Even when I'm freaked out that he might kill me!

But would he? I can tell that he's furious at me. What I can't tell is what he intends to do with me. Use me as his fucktoy, then kill me? Part of me finds it hard to believe that he would kill me, though maybe he wouldn't actually pull the trigger himself. Or maybe he would. I clearly don't know him as well as I thought I did.

He's a *gangster*. His cousin had my roommate Amy *murdered*.

The heels I wear have been doing their version of homicide on my feet, and I can no longer find a position for my standing foot that is discernibly less painful. I should never have allowed myself to be talked into buying these shoes. I shouldn't have gone on that date with Josh. Coretta had taken my son, Evan, with her to her daughter's house for the weekend so that I could study, not go out and wind up kidnapped by my ex.

Stop it! I tell myself. Crying over spilled milk isn't going to help me out of my current predicament.

I tug against my bonds again, but they don't give any more than before. If I can't get out of these ropes, I have no hope. I'm a sitting duck.

So I have to find a way to get untied. I had suggested to Darren that I would give him a blow job. He'd passed on it at the time, but he had also said, "Don't worry. You'll get a chance to blow me."

That suggests he will let me blow him. Problem is, there are many ways he can have me give him head. I could still be trapped in rope. But my current position wouldn't work, and when he undoes the ropes to change things up, I might have a chance then.

Ideally, I would have my hands free. Then I could maybe grab something for a weapon.

Looking around, I see only the light bulb and a chair against the wall nearest me. Otherwise, this basement is only concrete flooring, windowless walls, and exposed pipes. I think about my shoes. Maybe the heels could work as a weapon? But how good would they work against a gun?

I shiver, remembering the shot I heard earlier. And Darren isn't alone. I'm not sure who the others could be. Maybe Marshall, his sometime bodyguard and head of security.

But one thing or one person at a time. Maybe I'll get lucky. I have to try something. And I'm not afraid of getting shot or hurt. As long as I can make it out alive. For Evan. There's no way I'm dying and leaving him without a mother when he's already missing a father.

Taking a large breath, I tamp down the fear that occasionally swells inside of me. I need focus and calm.

It feels like an eternity before I finally hear footsteps coming down the stairs. Thank God. I wouldn't have an ankle left if I had to wait another minute. Or arms, which are sore from being raised above me for so long. My mouth is completely dry thanks to my own panties stuffed here. And because I'm still occasionally nursing and pumping, my breasts feel tight and uncomfortable.

37

Meanwhile, there's still the faintest simmer of desire between my legs, thanks to the crotch rope.

Please let it be Darren.

The door opens, and I breathe a silent sigh of relief when I see Darren standing at the threshold. Even in a simple pair of jeans and a loose-fitting tank that reveals his muscular arms and parts of his chiseled chest, he looks hot as hell. Physically, he hasn't changed all that much, whereas I've put on a few pounds. The main visible change is that he's grown a faint stubble, giving him a rugged quality. In more ordinary and non-threatening circumstances, if he didn't turn out to be a gangster, I might have told him I liked the new look.

He sets down a suitcase before walking over. Taking the panties out of my mouth, he asks, "How we doing, Bridge

I really want something to drink, but I put that need aside and brace myself for the performance of a lifetime. I have zero experience in acting, but I've got to qualify for an Oscar now.

"Mercy, sir," I reply, wanting relief from the bondage and the crotch rope.

He lifts a brow. "That's funny. You think you get a fucking safe word?"

My heart accelerates, and I try not to let fear grip me too tightly. No safe words? We've never played without safe words before. But that's actually not the issue. There was a time I would have trusted Darren enough to go without safe words. It's his anger that scares me.

I lower my eyes. "I'm sorry, sir."

He tugs on the crotch rope, making me gasp as the knot rubs further into my clit.

"I could have you wear this all day," he says.

"Yes, sir."

The muscle about his jaw tightens. "That all you've got to say?"

What does he want me to say? I could tell him I want to suck him off, but the timing doesn't feel right. It might come off disingenuous.

"I-I deserve to be punished?" I try.

"You bet the fuck you do."

I swallow with difficulty. He releases the rope and caresses my flesh.

"So how should you be punished?"

A thought crosses my mind. "Depends."

"On what?"

"Where we are," I answer. "There's a BDSM club in downtown Denver. If we're not too far…"

"We're too far."

"How far?"

He stares at me. I think he knows I'm trying to figure out our location.

He folds his arms in front of him. "What's this BDSM club called?"

"Club Kink."

"You been there?"

I shake my head.

"Then how do you know about it?"

"I was bored one day and was curious if Denver had that kind of scene."

"I don't believe you. How often did you play there?"

"I've never been there," I insist truthfully. Even though I had looked it up, I couldn't imagine playing with anyone but Darren.

He shakes his head. "I used to think you were such a goody two-shoes, someone trustworthy. Guess I was wrong. I hate being wrong."

My toes come off the floor as he pulls the crotch rope up.

"Now let's get back to your punishment," he says. "Why don't you start off with some ideas?"

Inwardly, I groan. I don't want to answer his question. There are so many things that he can do, so many options in his arsenal. Bastinado is probably my least favorite, so I don't want to offer up that suggestion. But he'll know if I'm trying to lowball my punishment.

As if impatient for an answer, he tugs the crotch rope even higher.

"Nipple clamps?" I yelp. "A clothespin zipper? Making me blow you for hours on end?"

"Not bad. Let's do them all. Along with my ideas, of course."

My stomach feels queasy, but I'm encouraged that I'll get to do the fellatio.

Stepping behind me, he unties my leg. My

standing foot is so happy to have the other foot bear my weight for a change.

"Squat down," he orders as he loosens the rope above my wrists.

I lower myself. He pushes me till my butt is touching my ankles, then spreads my thighs wide. With the cord of rope in his hands, he binds my upper leg to my calves. He retrieves another cord of rope and does the same to my other leg. With both legs bent and bound, I can't run. The position pushes more of my weight towards my toes. I really wish I had never bought these damn shoes. I may refuse to wear heels the rest of my life.

Darren undoes the rope from the pipes, but instead of freeing my wrists like I had hoped, he anchors the end of the rope to the crotch rope. My wrists, no longer pulled above me, are now secured behind my neck, stretching my triceps.

Squatting down to face me, he reaches between my thighs and touches me, a finger on each side of the rope, teasing me. Unfulfilled desire from before percolates in anticipation. Taking hold of the knot, he wiggles it against my clit. My breath quickens. I should not be wanting this.

After he's worked me up, he stands and undoes his jeans. "Now you can blow me."

I stare at the semi-erect cock he pulls out. He came once already, so it may take a while to get him to come again. I just hope my body can survive being tied up for the duration.

"Come on, Bridge," he urges, waving his erection in front of me.

I open my mouth wide, like a baby bird for its meal. He slaps his shaft against me, deliberately missing my mouth. I try my best to catch him. He lets me. My lips close about his hardness. I tongue the underside of his cock and suck till my cheeks cave in.

Putting a hand on the top of my head, he pushes me down his length. I start to gag when he goes too far. I haven't done this in over two years. He pulls my head back, then pushes me back down even farther this time. My body resists, and I try my best to relax and adjust. When we were together, he always gave me a respite. It wasn't always as much as I wanted, but it was enough to gather my bearings. But there's no relief this time. I choke and cough on him. My body retches when his cock hits the back of my throat.

He finally gives me a second to catch my breath, right before he shoves my face into his groin, grinding my nose into his pubic hair. I sputter and gag. My eyes water.

He yanks me off his cock. A web of spittle falls from his cock to my chin.

Holding me by the hair at the top of my head, he asks, "That what you wanted?"

After my body has calmed, I reply, "Yes, sir."

"You missed my cock, didn't you?" he asks, tapping it against my cheek and over my eye.

"Yes, sir."

Reaching behind me, he tugs on the rope connecting my wrists to the crotch rope. The knot rubs against my clit. Ever so slightly, it takes my mind off how sore my feet, legs, arms, and mouth are. But he doesn't do this for long. Straightening, he plunges himself back into my mouth.

"Harder," he orders.

I suck harder, channeling my frustration and lack of fulfillment into giving him as much head as I can. He groans and starts pumping his hips. I'm able to get into a rhythm and ensure my lips wrap him as tightly as possible while I go up and down. I want him to remember how good I can make him feel. I want to see his brow furrow in pleasure. I want to see his body surrender, to know what I can do to him.

Though I'd rather take a break, I press on. Up and down his cock. Up and down. Sucking and sucking. Until he starts bucking into my face faster and faster. I try to keep up, doing what I can to keep the gagging at a minimum.

With a roar, he pulls out and unloads over my face and chest. The white viscous liquid lands on my lashes, my cheek and lips. Part of me feels triumphant that I got him to come and relieved that he's no longer pounding into my mouth and throat. But now what? I'm still tied up and unable to gain my freedom.

After sending the final spurt of cum onto my

dress, he lefts my chin. "Don't worry, Bridge. I'm not done with you. Not by a long shot."

CHAPTER FIVE

BRIDGET
Past

After arriving at The Lotus with Amy and being told that Darren is in a meeting, I decide to say hi to Felipe, the bartender with the friendly smile and about the only person who didn't treat me like a leper for not wearing an outfit swank enough for the club my first time here.

"Anything ever work out with that hot stockbroker?" I ask Felipe as I straddle a barstool.

Felipe, in the middle of fixing me a Shirley Temple, stops to gush. "OMG, Bryan is the best. We've gone out three times since that night you helped set us up."

"I didn't set you up."

"Yes, you did. If you hadn't talked to that woman and found out he wasn't on a date with her, I wouldn't have had the guts to talk to him."

"I'm glad things are working out."

"He's soooo dreamy. I usually hate the way I

look in the morning, you know, before I've put on a little foundation, but he says I look beautiful."

I smile. "Sounds like a nice guy."

He hands me my drink. "So...how are things with you and Darren?"

"Me and Darren?"

"Don't act all innocent with me. I noticed you going up in the elevator with him last time, and I didn't see you again before I closed everything down."

I blush and sip my drink, then decide to confide in Felipe. "He invited me to Phuket. I thought I heard wrong at first. Is that an everyday thing for him?"

Felipe raises his brows. "Not really. JD's sister is getting married there next week."

"Going to a family event sounds like a big deal, but I doubt that Darren sees it as serious."

I try to get a read on Felipe's reaction but don't see anything. So I ask, "How long have you worked for Darren?"

"I've been here since The Lotus opened."

"Is he a nice boss?"

"I have no complaints."

"Anything else I should know about him?"

Felipe, looking down at the bar, doesn't respond right away.

"Don't worry. I'm not gonna tell on you," I assure him.

Felipe still hesitates.

Not wanting my question to dampen our still-young camaraderie, I say, "It's okay. You don't have to say anything. If I'm just the flavor of the month, I can take it. I'm a big girl."

He smiles, but it's an odd smile, like the kind you'd give a kid who asks you if everything is okay when everything is *not* okay.

"I like your cold-shoulder top," he says, "though it's not as memorable as that sweater you wore before."

"You should see the puff jacket I left in the coat check. It's pistachio colored."

His jaw drops.

I laugh. "And this top actually isn't mine. It belongs to my housemate, Simone."

This is the third time I've borrowed clothes from her. The first was a jumpsuit I wore to a fundraiser Darren hosted for Eric Drumm's father. The second was a black halter dress I wore to The Lotus and then Darren's residence above the club.

"Thanks for the drink," I say before hopping off to head to the restroom.

I wonder why Felipe had the reaction that he did to my questions. Was I being too prying? Is it because Darren's a player, and out of loyalty to his boss, he doesn't want to say anything bad? Well, I'm not like Amy. I'm not going to fall head over heels for Darren just because I'm sexually attracted to him. Super sexually attracted.

Deep in my own thoughts, I accidentally bump

into a woman while heading for the stalls.

"Oh! Sorry!" I apologize.

She continues on her way, heading in the opposite direction of the entry/exit. Noticing that she dropped something, I pick it up. It's a clothespin. A fancy one painted black and with rhinestones.

"You dropped this," I call out to her.

I follow her to the exit on the other side of the restroom. I've noticed this other way out before and figured it was for staff. I step out of the restroom and into…another club? This one is swathed in red pulsing light, and the patrons are…

Holy shit.

CHAPTER SIX

BRIDGET
Past

*I*s this what Felipe was hesitant to talk about? I wonder as I stare agog at a naked woman tied down to a table in the middle of the floor. On her nipples, she has clamps connected by a thin chain. An equally naked man is thrusting himself into her while tugging on the chain. She groans and grunts, "Please, Master, please let me come." A minute later, he tells her to come, which she does, her whole body trembling as her head falls back with a thump against the table.

A different type of music throbs low in this part of the building. There's no DJ that I can tell. Instead, I see, in a darker corner of the room, a dominatrix wearing a dark purple mask over her eyes pegging a man bent over the back of a chair. He thanks her repeatedly. A few patrons, some dressed in club attire, others more scantily clad, lounge on sofas or at tables, taking in the activities around them. Looking up to the second-floor balcony, I find two women kissing each other. I feel like I shouldn't be watching all this, but these people don't seem to mind onlookers.

Deciding I'm definitely in the wrong part of the club, I take a step back and bump into something.

Darren.

I flush, even though he should be the one embarrassed that I've discovered the secret side of The Lotus.

"Now you've seen the whole club," Darren remarks with nonchalance.

"Yeah," is all I can come up with.

Behind me, I hear a woman cry, "Yes, fuck me, please!"

I turn around, an instinctive reaction to someone screaming. A very flexible woman lies upon a rug, holding both her legs to her chest, while another woman wearing a dildo penetrates her. I watch as her lips purse and pleasure fills her face.

Turning back to Darren, I ask, "This go on every night here?"

"Some nights are quieter, others louder," he replies, his gaze boring into me.

"It's hard to imagine louder," I reply as the woman on the rug shouts at her partner to go harder.

Darren takes me by the elbow. "Let's sit down."

What? He wants us to stay here?

He leads me to a small dining table. I take a seat

tentatively. A server wearing a leather teddy and over-the-knee boots comes up and asks if we would like something to drink.

"There are no alcoholic drinks on this side of the club," Darren says, "but that's not really an issue for you, is it?"

I shake my head. "I'm fine. Felipe made me a Shirley Temple just a few minutes ago."

Darren tells the server to bring us some water. "You waiting until you're officially twenty-one to graduate to adult drinks?"

"I like my kid's drinks, and Felipe makes a mean Shirley Temple."

He chuckles while shaking his head. He makes a comment, but I'm distracted because I've spotted the woman from the restroom in an alcove beneath the second-floor balcony. Only now she's naked, her wrists tied above her to a wooden post, and she's covered with clothespins matching the one I found.

Darren follows my gaze. "Something the matter?"

"She dropped one back in the restroom," I reply, showing him the one I hold.

"Return it to her Dom."

I look at the beefy man with a hood over his head standing before the woman wearing nothing but clothespins. I'm not exactly eager to interact with the patrons on this side of the club, but I should return the clothespin. Getting up, I walk over.

Holding up the clothespins, I say to the hooded man, "I think this might be hers."

"Thank you," he says in a surprisingly cordial manner.

I don't know why I assumed a man in a hood wouldn't be well-mannered.

He accepts the clothespin. His other hand holds the end of a string that seems to run through the other clothespins.

"Would you like to do the unzipping?" he asks.

I wave "no" with both my hands. "I'm just here to return the clothespin."

Quickly, I make my way back to the table and take a good guzzle of the water that has just been placed there. Maybe I shouldn't wait till I'm actually twenty-one to try alcohol.

"What did he say?" Darren asked.

"He asked me if I wanted to do the unzipping?" I reply.

"You didn't want to?"

"I don't even know what he's talking about."

"Watch."

The man applies the clothespin I gave him by pinching the flesh of her belly. He asks the woman a question. She nods. A second later, she's screaming as he yanks the string and pulls off all the clothespins.

"Oh my God," I gasp.

Darren stares at me. Hard. "This your first time in a BDSM club?"

I turn my widened eyes to him. "Um, hell yeah."

How many people does he know who can answer that question negatively? This is crazy. Darren is casually sitting here like we're in a coffee shop. What made him think I had any experience with BDSM whatsoever?

"You know anything about BDSM?" he asks.

I shake my head.

"You must have read about it. I'm told it's a popular genre for women."

"I don't get around to reading a lot of fiction. Even if I did, I don't think I'd pick up a book with BDSM in it."

"Why not?"

"Because...why would I want to read about pain?"

"Because it's sexy."

I cock a brow to show my skepticism.

"Why else do you think people do it?" he returns.

"I can think of better ways to get off than resorting to pain."

"How do you know until you've tried it?"

"It just seems...wrong."

"Part of its appeal." He leans over the table. "I won't say there aren't people who play for the wrong reasons, people who have deep psychological wounds that they're reliving through BDSM, but for the rest of us, it's just fun."

My breath catches in my chest. "So you're a...participant of BDSM?"

He gazes intensely into my eyes, like he's trying to dig up something. "Not just a participant. I'm a hardcore fan."

"Oh." As I process how I feel about this revelation, I ask, "How long have you, um, been a participant?"

"Since college. There were these girls in my dorm who were nuts about *Fifty Shades,* so JD and I looked into it."

"JD is into it, too?"

I think about Amy and how she hurts easily. She says that's why she never did sports, too much potential for injury.

"Not lately," he replies.

I breathe a sigh of relief for Amy before asking, "And has this always been a part of The Lotus?"

"Yes."

He's serious about this BDSM stuff. I really don't know how I feel about that. I watch as the hooded man jams a vibrator between the woman's legs. She comes in less than a minute.

"Pain can jack up adrenaline," Darren explains, "making orgasms more intense. Couple that with the endorphins from arousal and you can get a pretty amazing high."

Still skeptical, I say, "I'll stick to plain old sex for now."

He smiles as he sits back in his chair.

"What?"

"I like how you said 'for now.'"

I probably should have followed that up with saying that I would never give BDSM a try, but for some reason, the idea is not as horrifying as I would have thought. In fact, I'm curious about it.

The woman tied to the post is having another orgasm. Already.

CHAPTER SEVEN

DARREN
Past

*F*uck. I did not expect this.

Unless I'm with a woman who I know plays in kink, I usually gauge a woman's interest with something tamer, like spanking, rough sex, or tying her up and tormenting her nipples with pinching and biting.

But I spilled everything once Bridget walked over to the other side of The Lotus. I didn't have to, but for some reason, I felt okay doing so with Bridget. Maybe it's because she didn't look completely horrified by what she saw. She even seemed a little intrigued.

I can see the wheels turning in her head. Deciding not to overwhelm her with too much at her first encounter with BDSM, I suggest we head back to JD and Amy, who might be wondering where her friend had gone off to, though I suspect she might be too far gone in her mojito and JD to give much thought to Bridget.

Back at my spot on the regular side of the club, I see that I'm right. JD and Amy are making out on the sofa like teenagers in the back of a movie theater. I was about to tell her we should head up to my residence, but she might have second thoughts now that she knows I'm into BDSM.

"You hungry?" I ask her. "I can have food brought up to my place. Come on."

She glances over at JD and Amy, then follows me. We turn and head down the stairs, bumpy into Manny on the way.

"JD up there?" Manny asks. "Was hoping I could talk to him."

"He's with someone," I answer.

"I'll be quick."

"You should wait. Or call him. That'll be best."

Taking Bridget by the elbow, I continue on our way. Finding a server, I tell him to have the chef send up a few dishes.

"Your chef must have a long day between making breakfast and serving food late at night," Bridget remarks.

"I have a different chef for breakfast and lunch."

"Oh, that makes sense."

We step into the elevator. She's quiet in thought. Probably still processing what she saw.

I yank her to me as the doors close, cup the side of her face, and smother her mouth with mine. Energy surges between us. I devour her mouth. She doesn't pull away. I wasn't a hundred percent sure she wouldn't. The kiss is a test, and I'm encouraged that the BDSM hasn't scared her off. Yet.

Watching Bridget taking in what went on in the other side of the club has strengthened my ardor. Soon, I'm working her mouth so hard, she couldn't tear herself away if she wanted to. She gets a reprieve when the elevator doors open. But not for long. I hoist her over my shoulder.

"I can walk on my own two feet," she says after I've stepped out of the elevator.

I walk up to the facial recognition device that unlocks my door. It's an unnecessary precaution, but Marshall insisted if I didn't want to have someone posted outside my door.

"I don't need that much protection," I had explained to Marshall.

The son of a US Army lieutenant who married an ethnic Chinese woman when he was stationed at Camp Humphreys in South Korea, Marshall looks more like his tall, dark father than his paler, more diminutive mother. At 6'4" and 245 pounds, he's actually larger than his father.

"I'm not involved in any of the major triad businesses," I had added.

"Your father was. And he had himself a few enemies," Marshall had responded. "And your mother called me."

I had stopped there. I'm sure Marshall didn't want to be harassed any more than I did by my worry-prone mother.

Once inside my residence, I head straight for the bedroom and dump her on the bed, which has been turned down. My mouth is back on hers. How does she taste so good? And feel so good. The smallest motions of her body beneath mine send my desire skyrocketing. She wraps her arms about me, one hand running through my hair. As I plunge my tongue into her mouth, my hips press into her, seeking relief for my hard-on.

In the back of my head, I realize, not counting the foot massage, that this is the third time I'm having sex with Bridget. I don't do it with anyone more than twice if it's just for fun. Maybe I should make the rule three times instead of two. Because there's no way I'm backing off with Bridget now. I'm dying to know if she would be willing to go beyond vanilla. We did some breath play back at her place, but it wasn't something she had acquiesced to upfront. She had come good, though.

Finding her hands a little distracting, I pull her top up and over her head, but not her arms. The tight top traps her limbs nicely. I look over her black lace bra. Not bad, though it still looks more Fruit of the Loom than Victoria's Secret. Pushing up the bra, I grope a breast. She tries to wriggle out of her top, stopping when I pinch a nipple.

"Um, are we—is this part of BDSM?" she asks.

"You'll know without question when we're in BDSM territory," I tell her as I go back to kneading a breast. "For one, you'd have a safe word."

She seems to breathe a sigh of relief. "So we'd only go there if I consented?"

"Yes."

And you'll consent. Hell, you won't just consent to it. You'll beg for it.

I roll her nipple between my thumb and forefinger and lightly tug on it before applying my mouth. She gasps and writhes with every lick, suck and nibble. After coming off the bud, I give the side of the breast a light slap. Looking into her eyes, I don't see much of a reaction. No alarm. I go to work on her other nipple as lustfully as I did her mouth while groping the other breast. I pull the bra over her head and behind her, further locking her upper arms to her body, then give her a reprieve when I lightly kiss my way down to her jeans. I cup her crotch and rub her through the denim. Her wetness has seeped through to her pants.

Ignoring the tension in my own groin, I slowly unbutton and unzip her jeans before inching them down past her hips. I leave them wrapped about her thighs and breathe in the scent of her arousal. My blood pumps faster, but I stifle the urge to maul her. Instead, I sit down beside her and tuck my hand into her panties. She moans when my fingers connect with her clit.

"So what did you think about the rest of my club?" I ask as I leisurely caress her flesh.

"You mean...um...the...um...BDSM?" she asks, clearly distracted by my fondling.

"You know what it stands for?"

She furrows her brow. "B-Bondage... Domination... Sadism and Masochism?"

"The 'D' can also stand for Discipline and the 'S' for Submission. The acronym covers a lot." Her lashes flutter as I find a poignant spot on her clit. "You didn't seem scared."

"I didn't?"

"Maybe a little."

Leaning over, I capture a nipple between my teeth. I torment the hardened nub while my fingers rub her more aggressively. With her arms trapped slightly behind her sides by her top and bra and her legs trapped by her jeans, she squirms like a worm on a hook.

"There's nothing to worry about. We'll take it slow," I tell her.

"What?" she asks breathlessly.

I curl two fingers into her snatch. Her eyes widen as she groans. Pulling out my digits, I spread her juices over her clit. She whimpers. I continue to jerk her off. Her panties are a puddle of wetness.

"Ask to come," I say.

"Wh-what?"

"Do you want to come?"

The look on her face tells me how lame she regards my question, but she doesn't realize I'm starting her training.

"You want to come?" I ask again, slowing my caresses so she focuses better.

"Yeah."

"Then ask to come."

She looks slightly bewildered. "Like, 'can I come?'"

"Just like that."

My fingers slow to a stop.

Her brow furrows, but she asks, "Can I come?"

I resume the ministrations. "Yes, you can come. Come good, Bridge."

A minute later she comes undone, her eyes closed, her body quivering. I smile to myself. She passed the first test with flying colors.

CHAPTER EIGHT

BRIDGET
Past

I'm not sure how I feel about having my arms pinioned like this, but who the hell cares? When Darren strokes my clit the way he does, all I want to do is let him work his magic. The orgasm is good, though not as explosive as the last time. Every time he tongued or sucked my nipple, a current would zip to the area between my legs. When he had slowed down while talking, I wanted to grind myself into his hand like crazy. I don't remember exactly what we were talking about, and before the mist of my orgasm has faded enough for me to recall, I'm flipped onto my stomach and my hips pulled to the edge of the bed.

"Don't move," Darren says before giving my butt a swat.

I watch him grab a condom from the drawer of his bedside table. Whew. With my arms pinned to my body, I can't exactly defend myself if he tries to go without protection. Looking back, it probably wasn't very smart of me to fall into sex so soon without knowing Darren well enough. I let lust get the better of me, and I never thought I would. I'm lucky that Darren isn't one of those creeps who do that messed-up stealthing shit.

I hear his buckle coming undone, the zipper of his pants, and then the crinkle of the condom wrapper. Just to be sure, I twist my head around to see that the condom is actually on. It is. He pulls his shirt off, and I glimpse his chest, still gorgeously tan.

"You did good, Bridge," he says as he pulls my underwear and jeans down to my knees.

He slides himself between my legs and sinks into me, filling me with his hardness.

Oh God, that feels good.

He leans over me and murmurs near my ear, "You're so sexy when you ask to come."

I blush. That's right. I did that.

He manages to sink his erection deeper. "Do it again."

"Ask to come?" I verify.

He starts rolling his hips, making me quiver in anticipation. My body is already up for orgasm #2.

"Ask to come," he confirms.

"May I come?"

He drives his hips into my backside. "May I come, *sir.*"

"May I come, sir!"

64

The words tumble from my mouth before I have time to think. This is part of BDSM, isn't it?

"Not yet," he replies.

What the hell? Not yet?

"I asked nicely," I reply.

He laughs. "I didn't say you couldn't. Just hold off a little."

Like there's anything he can do to stop me. But if he wants to play this game, I guess I'll go along because I want that orgasm.

He thrusts with the perfect motion, with finesse, not too fast that I can't appreciate how good it feels or slow enough to drive me crazy. And the angle of penetration hits that sweet but jarring spot, stroking a delicious urgency. Is he good or just lucky? Doesn't matter. I groan with need, with pleasure, with gratitude.

"Oh my God," I mumble against the bed as I feel my climax coming to a crest.

"Not yet."

"Hmm?"

"I didn't say you could come yet."

It doesn't matter what he says. My body's going to do what it's going to do.

Or not.

Darren has stopped thrusting. My body's confused. His length flexes inside me, and my pussy clenches down on him, seeking to unleash the rapture.

Come on...fuck me.

But there's no motion. Only silence.

Finally, Darren asks, "You were about to come,

weren't you?"

I bury my face into the bed. "Yeah."

He bites my earlobe and growls, "You come when I say you can."

Abruptly, he pulls out, pulls off my boots and yanks off my jeans and underwear before flipping me onto my back. He throws my right leg over his shoulder and plunges himself back into me. Holding my leg against him, he rolls his hips.

I quiver with need. "Okay...can I come now?"

He only stares at me, his eyes dark with desire.

"Please," I add.

He continues to rock against me, stoking the flames swirling in my groin. The sensations are better than any rush from sugar or chocolate. I'm so close to erupting. But he hasn't actually said I can come yet.

Holding back the wave of ecstasy, I manage to stutter, "So, I c-can come?"

"Almost."

Almost?! I can only do so much.

"Now, Bridge."

With his free hand, he rubs my clit while sinking himself deep into me. The pressure I tried to hold back explodes, sending shudders through me from head to toe. I have no control of my body as it bucks and quakes. For several seconds, I can't even scream. Darren shoves his hips, his pelvis smacking into my derriere fast and furious before he, too, climaxes. I feel his erection throb inside of me. The sensation sends little pulses down my legs.

Even after he's pulled out, I remain where I am

to recover, waiting for my body to return to equilibrium. As I emerge from the bliss, I wonder to myself, did I just call him "Sir?"

CHAPTER NINE

DARREN
Past

I look over at Bridget and consider flipping her back onto her stomach. I liked how she looked with her ass rounding the edge of the bed. There's still so much I can do to her in that position.

But the food's probably waiting by the front door.

After tossing the condom and pulling up my pants, I plant kisses from her belly to her mouth. Her words—*may I come, sir*—still ring deliciously in my ears. Sitting her up, I pull her bra and top down her arms.

"You want your clothes back or something else to wear?" I ask, picking her jeans and panties off the floor.

She looks at the clothes I lay upon the bed. "I'll take something else."

From my dresser, I pull out a pair of black silk

pajamas. They'll be too large on her since they're mine, but the bottoms are drawstring. Or she could just wear the top.

"You don't mind?" she asks after I hand her the pajamas. "These feel really nice."

"Put them on," I reply, wanting to see her in my pajamas for some reason.

After buttoning on the top and slipping on the bottoms, she fiddles with the loose drawstrings. I step in and yank the drawstrings tight before tying them. She looks good in my pajamas.

"These are nice," she said, feeling the sleeve. "You might not get them back."

I cup her jaw and grin. "I'll have fun trying."

Her lips part in an irresistible manner. I close them with mine, savoring how soft and responsive they are. There'll be time for more later.

"You said you were hungry," I say, releasing her before I walk out of the bedroom.

"Actually, I didn't," she responds. "You asked me if I was, then said you could have food brought up to your place before I could really answer."

I pause. Is that right? Probably. Women don't usually dispute my game plan.

"So you're not hungry?" I ask.

"I'll eat," she replies.

Opening the front door, I find a cart waiting. I wheel it in to the dining table. Removing the lids, I see that the chef sent up lobster pot stickers with ginger-scallion sauce, Kobe beef sliders with black truffles, and a forbidden rice pudding with mango.

69

Eying the food, Bridget sits down next to the head of the table. "Now I'm hungry."

"Dig in," I tell her and pop the cork of a bottle of zinfandel that came with the food. I pour two glasses.

"Oh, I don't drink," she reminds me.

"This is nothing like *baijiu.* It's fruity."

She hesitates.

"What are you afraid of?" I ask. "That you'll get drunk, and I'll take advantage of you?"

"Maybe I'm worried you might pull some of that BDSM on me."

I could point out that I already have, but instead I reassure her, "I don't play with intoxicated subs."

"That's responsible of you."

"They can't fully appreciate the pain if they're drunk."

She frowns. I chuckle.

"I'm good with water," she says, taking one of the bottles of mineral water and pouring it into a glass.

"You always a rule follower?" I ask.

"Depends on the rule. Some rules need to be broken, and the world needs rule breakers, like Rosa Parks or Susan B. Anthony."

"And you think the drinking age is important enough that you can't break it? In most of the world, you can drink once you're eighteen. The US has one of the highest age requirements, but it has more alcohol-related problems than most of the world."

"Yeah, we're pretty underdeveloped in a lot of ways."

"You're not going to get arrested for having a sip of wine. If I dragged you down to a police station to have you arrested, they'd kick us out for wasting their time."

"They might arrest you, though, for serving alcohol to a minor, though I turn twenty-one in just two months. It's not that I think the drinking age is a rule that shouldn't be broken, but I've made it this far, why break my streak?"

"How have you made it this far? Weren't you ever curious?"

She shrugs. "Not really. My grandmother didn't drink. Growing up, I saw one of my neighbor's sons acting stupid when he was drunk. He then hurled all over our walkway."

"But you're in college now. You don't drink at frat parties?"

"I don't go to a lot of frat parties. Did you when you were at UCLA?"

"No. Most of the frat guys I came across were assholes."

"I've met some nice ones, but Greek organizations do seem to draw a lot of assholes."

Setting down her water, she tries a pot sticker. "Wow, these are to die for."

I sit down at the head of the table and watch her eat. The look on her face reminds me of how she looked a few moments ago in the throes of her orgasm. I always get a kick watching her come.

"How are you not five hundred pounds, eating like this?" she asks.

It's a rhetorical question, so I move on to more pressing matters. "You never sent me your photo."

"Okay, about that," she says, helping herself to a slider next. "You weren't serious about Phuket, Thailand."

"You think I'm joking?"

I sit back and watch her eyes light up after a bite of the slider. Either she loves food or she doesn't feed herself well enough. I've never been so fascinated watching a woman eat before. The few times Kimberly would indulge in something like dessert, she'd complain the whole time about how she'd either have to work out extra hard at the gym afterward or, if she felt lazy, induce vomiting.

Bridget raises a brow. "You invite women to international destinations regularly?"

"I don't," I admit. "But it just so happens I have to be in Phuket."

"Because of a wedding?"

"Yeah, who told you that?"

"Felipe."

"You getting chummy with my bartender?"

"He was the only one nice to me my first time at the club."

I like Felipe. He's not a member of the *Jing San* and probably knows more than he should, but he's always been discreet. Still, I'm surprised that he's chatty with Bridget so soon after meeting her.

"So are you attending a wedding?" Bridget asks.

"Is that a big deal?" I return.

Maybe I should have thought it through more before inviting Bridget. A wedding is a family event, and that might send the wrong signal to her, that our relationship is more serious than it is.

"It's not like I'm taking you home to meet my folks," I add. "My father's dead. And my mom's not likely to attend."

"I wasn't expecting anything like that. I don't think I'd be ready to meet your folks yet, anyway."

What does that mean? Is she relieved that our relationship doesn't appear to be moving too fast?

"Maybe flying off to Thailand isn't a big deal for you," she continues, "but I don't get invitations like that. Ever."

"Then it's your lucky day. I have to be at a wedding in about a week. I get a plus one. It happens to be in Thailand."

"And I'd love to go, but Thailand is a little out of my budget."

"You think I'd invite you to Thailand and make you pay for it?"

"Well, I didn't want to assume."

All the women I've ever been with wouldn't have assumed anything else.

She eyes the dessert. "Mind if I dig in?"

"'Course not."

She takes a spoonful and her eyes widen. She lets the mouthful linger, chewing slowly before swallowing. Warmth stirs in my groin. Yeah, I've got to fuck her soon.

"The thing is," she says, "I also have school, I have an internship, and I have a job."

She's declining a date to Phuket? What's the matter with this woman?

As if sensing my disconcertion, she adds, "I mean, it's super generous of you, and I wish I could go..."

"Can't you get class notes from a classmate or catch the lectures online?" I ask.

"My health policy seminar is discussion based. Participation is part of the grade. And it's not that I can't take time off from my job and internship, but a week is short notice."

I stare at her, floored. I can't tell if it's really logistics and a strong sense of responsibility that holds her back or something else.

"If you didn't have to worry about school or work, would you go?" I ask.

"I guess."

She guesses? I expected a much more positive answer.

"You guess," I echo.

"Letting a guy pay for dinner is one thing, paying for a trip to Thailand is...different."

"Not to me."

"Still, I'd feel guilty about it."

74

Why should you feel guilty? I want to ask. But another thought comes to mind. "Would you feel better if you could pay for it?"

"Sure."

"All right. I'll let you pay for it."

She does a double-take. "What?"

"Not with money," I clarify.

"Then with what?"

Heat tingles through me. "A night at my club. The *other* side of my club."

CHAPTER TEN

BRIDGET
Past

My body is so drawn to Darren, I'm actually considering his proposal. Which is crazy because I haven't known him for that long.

Stalling, I take another spoonful of the creamy rice dessert infused with tropical fruit. This food is crazy amazing.

I dare to meet his penetrating gaze, which feels like it sees everything.

"That's if I were to go," I demur.

His countenance darkens a little, but he doesn't look too hurt that I'm declining his invitation.

"What's stopping you?" he inquires.

"What I listed before—school, work."

He leans back in his chair and props an ankle on the opposite knee. "People call in sick to work on short notice."

"But I'm not sick."

"Don't tell me you've never lied before."

I balk. "Not on something like this."

He studies me like I'm some strange insect he's never seen before. "Who's going to get hurt if you lie? It's a victimless crime, and it's not even a crime."

"It doesn't matter. Actually, my conscience would be the victim. I wouldn't be able to enjoy myself in Phuket knowing I had lied to go."

He shakes his head. "Fine. But if you were sick, you wouldn't have a problem calling in sick without any notice, right?"

"Sure."

"And your job would make do without your presence, right?"

"Yeah."

"They aren't going to fall to pieces because you were absent a week."

"'Course not."

"So tell them you'll be gone a week. You just agreed your job would survive without you."

"It's not that easy," I argue. "Getting sick isn't the same thing as flying off to Thailand. If I'm sick, I'm physically incapacitated and possibly contagious. And it's not my choice to get sick. Taking a vacation is selfish and might be viewed as irresponsible."

"Might. How do you know it'll be seen as irresponsible? Maybe your boss will tell you you should jump at the chance to go on your first international trip."

I hadn't considered that possibility.

"What's your job anyway?" he asks.

"I work at one of the campus libraries processing returns and re-shelving books."

"So no one's going to die if you miss a week of work."

"A mountain of unprocessed books could fall on top of someone."

He grins. "And that would be the worst thing to happen."

"I guess. Sure."

"You're not the only one who works at the library."

"I'm not."

"What if you got someone else to cover your shift?"

"Okay, that could work. But I have an internship."

"What's the worst that could happen there?"

"Personally, I could get fired."

"So how much income would you lose from that?"

"None. It's unpaid. But I like my internship. And we're in the midst of a major fundraising effort. Plus, we're short-staffed because one of the program coordinators is out on maternity leave."

"Can you do any of that work remotely?"

It's my turn to study him. Does he really want me to go to Phuket that badly, or is he just giving me a hard time? I think it's the latter.

"So tell me more about this wedding in Phuket," I stall, because even though Darren makes it sound simple, I'm not convinced. "Is it a younger or older sister of JD's who's getting married?"

"Younger," he replies as he finishes off his wine.

"Do you have any siblings?"

"No. JD is the closest thing to a brother for me."

"Coretta's kids were like older sisters to me. Even though I didn't have a dad and my mom wasn't around much, I still felt like I was part of a family."

"When was the last time you saw your mother?"

"My high school graduation. My grandmother offered to pay for her flight from Florida at the time. I don't think she would have come otherwise."

"That's harsh."

I shrug. "I think my mom was genuinely hard up."

Though it wasn't like my grandmother had a lot of extra income to spare, but I had overheard her talking to my mother on the phone, insisting that she had to be there for my graduation. My mother would have jumped at the chance to go to Phuket. Who knows, she might be there now with her latest millionaire boyfriend.

But I'm not my mother.

"You said your mom's not likely to attend the wedding?" I ask.

"She's looking after a sick relative in Singapore."

"That's nice of her. Do you get to see her much?"

He stares at me. "You always ask a guy so many questions?"

"You prefer that we just sit and eat in silence? Although, you're not even eating," I point out.

"I'm not hungry."

But the look he gives me suggests otherwise, only *I'm* the main course. I take another sip of the water. Part of me wishes I was drinking the wine instead. "I should check to see when Amy plans on heading back."

"You think she's not spending the night with JD?"

"I shouldn't assume. I'm just going to give her a quick call." But I realize I don't have my cellphone with me because I had to leave it with security. I was told by a bouncer my first time here that photos aren't allowed. I had thought it a strange policy for a nightclub, but now that I've seen the other side of the club, I understand.

Darren dials his cousin on his cell. "Bridge wants to speak to Amy."

He hands me the phone and I hear Amy say in between giggling, "Sorry, Bridge, I meant to call you but forgot. I'm on my way to JD's place. Hope that's okay."

What was I supposed to say? That it's not okay? Besides, this has happened before. She leaves with JD, and I'm left with Darren.

"So I'll see you tomorrow then?" I confirm.

"Yeah...tomorrow."

"Have fun."

"You, too."

With a final giggle, she hangs up.

"Amy's going to JD's place for the night," Darren says.

I hand his cell back to him. "Yep."

He grabs my wrist instead, making me drop the cell on the table, and yanks me to him. Pulling me onto his lap, he clasps the back of my head and crushes my mouth to his. Desire warms my body immediately. His mouth engulfs mine, and I'm fine with drowning in his kiss. In fact, I can't get enough. I thread my fingers through his hair and try to keep up.

He thrusts his free hand under the pajama top to cup a breast. I sigh into his lips as I feel his strong fingers press into my flesh. He takes his time, thoroughly going to town on my mouth, groping my breast, teasing the nipple till I whimper. Unlike some of my past experiences, where the guy needs to start some kind of humping action soon. Instead, it's me that starts grinding my pelvis into him, seeking to relieve the yearning between my legs.

Grabbing the back of my legs and without unlocking his lips from mine, he stands up and sets me on the table. We continue to kiss as he rubs my crotch. His pajama bottoms are damp there, and I feel slightly bad that I've soiled them, but one could argue that he started it. His hand both satiates and incites my need. I moan as desire coils in my belly.

He presses me down to the glass surface of the table, then pulls the shirt up above my head. Thinking he's going to take it off, I lift my arms, but he leaves it halfway, covering my face.

"Don't move," he says as he holds my wrists down with one hand.

His other hand wanders over my body—breast, nipple, rib, abdomen. I can't see anything through the pajama top, and the visual deprivation makes the sense of touch more poignant. He kneads a breast, then toys with the nipple until I'm squirming. Each time he tugs the hardened bud, the craving between my thighs throbs.

After pulling loose the drawstring, he slips his hand into the pants and combs his fingers through the hair at my mound before reaching for the wetness below. I gasp when he grazes my clit and softly moan as he strokes it. He rubs circles around the nub with his middle and forefinger. I groan when he hits the most sensitive spot, which he works until I'm a mess of desperation.

"Lift your hips," he directs.

I don't want him to stop for a second, but I do as he says. Still holding my wrists to the table with one hand, he pulls the pants off with his other. I'm cognizant that the food is still on the table, not far from me, which means I don't have a lot of room to maneuver. I lie still as he binds my wrists with one of the pant legs. I feel the fabric tug and hear him wrapping what's probably the other pant leg around something. A table leg or maybe the other captain's chair at the end of the table.

For a few minutes, I lie immobile, wondering what he's going to do next, hoping he'll go back to fondling my clit. What's he doing? Why is he waiting? Hello?

When I finally feel him, I gasp loudly. It's his mouth on my nipple. For some reason, my nipple feels more sensitive than before. Fireworks of need go off in my lower body as he nibbles and sucks. I want to bring my feet onto the table so that I can bend my knees, but there's probably not enough room as my butt is near the edge. Plus, I don't want to knock over a dish.

He kneads my breast as he tongues the nub. I'm not sure how much more attention my nipple can take. It's never had such prolonged action.

Finally, he stops and backhands the side of my breast.

The slap surprises me, but I'm quickly fixed on the hand that is now back between my legs, caressing my wet flesh. He teases my clit again. I make a sound that's part whimper, part purr.

"That feels good, doesn't it?" he asks.

"Yes," I groan, feeling the heat of my breath bounce off the fabric and back into my face.

"You mean, 'yes, sir.'"

"Yes, sir."

I did it again. The words just fell from my

mouth. Because I'm not really thinking. All I want is for him to release all the pent-up tension he's built inside me.

He bears down on my nipple again with his mouth while he fondles my clit more intently. I feel my orgasm bubbling toward the surface. But he stops before it has the chance to erupt. He slaps the side of my breast again. I have to collect myself. I had been so ready to come. Maybe I should have vocalized more. I don't want him to stop. I want him to keep going.

"I was so close to coming there," I say.

"Were you?" he asks in a way that has me wondering if he already knew that and *deliberately* left me hanging.

"Yes! Really close."

Maybe if he goes back to masturbating me right now, we won't lose too much momentum.

His cellphone buzzes. I hear him pick it up and start texting.

"I want your headshot," he says. "In case you're able to make Thailand work. That way we can get your passport application started."

"Um, okay. What about my coming?"

"What about it?"

"Can I? Please?"

CHAPTER ELEVEN

DARREN
Past

*M*y head swims hearing her plea. And the way she said "Yes, sir." So natural. So effortless. So goddamn sexy.

Through most of our discussion about how she could make Phuket work, I was thinking to myself why I should bother convincing her. If she doesn't want to go, it's no skin off my nose. But now I want her to go. So she's going, one way or another.

The text I had just received was from Cheryl confirming our contact can get a fake passport made in less than forty-eight hours, and a real one issued within five days for the right bribe.

After putting down my phone, I look over Bridget, lying naked across my dining table, her wrists tied above her to the back of the chair pushed up against the table. I adjust my hard-on, imagining I had a crop right now. I look over all the places I could land the implement: her belly, her thighs, her breasts.

"Please, sir?" she asks when I still haven't responded.

I smile to myself. She catches on fast. I knew she was smart, and not just because she goes to Berkeley.

Standing at the head of the table where her legs dangle off the edge, I push her thighs apart. One of them bumps into a dish, but nothing spills or falls. I take in the scent of her arousal before positioning myself at her crotch.

"Ah!" she exclaims in surprise when I press my tongue to her clit.

Slowly, I lick the flesh around her swollen bud before teasing it with the tip of my tongue. She releases a wispy moan. Over and over, I taste her, feeling desire throbbing in my groin with each passing second. Gradually, I apply myself to the spot that seems the most receptive at the moment. By the increased urgency in her groans, I can tell her climax is nearing. Her body tenses as she seeks the finish line, which I will let her cross. Just not this second.

Straightening, I shed my clothes.

"Your timing is...impeccable," she murmurs beneath the pajamas.

"Yeah?"

"I was so close to coming again."

"Good." I rip open a condom I had grabbed earlier and roll it onto my cock.

"You have something against me coming?"

"It's called edging," I explain.

She doesn't respond right away. I climb onto the table. I can still smell the scent of her on my lips, which makes my cock pulse with desire.

"How many more times are you going to go through with this edging?" she asks.

"How many more can you take?"

"Zero."

I chuckle before I brace myself over her body and rub the tip of my shaft along her clit. Her groan is deep and long.

"Please let me come this time," she pleads.

"How badly do you want to?"

"Really, really bad."

I agitate my cock faster against her clit, making her writhe and gasp.

"Bad enough to go to Phuket?"

She stills for a second. I let my cock slide down to her opening and press against it. She moans. After pushing a few inches into her and withdrawing, I repeat my question.

"I guess," she murmurs.

"Good. So you'll make it happen." I push into her, a little deeper this time.

"I'll try."

I agitate my cock over her clitoris and urethral opening. "That attitude isn't good enough."

She gasps and squirms. "I'll try my best!"

"Make it happen."

"Okay, okay! I'll make it happen!"

I plunge myself into her. Holy crap. Her heat embracing my cock feels fucking incredible. I start thrusting. The table isn't the most comfortable place to have sex, but I want her so bad, there's no way I'm moving us.

"You better be telling the truth," I say, slamming into her for emphasis.

She cries out. "Yes, yes!"

I roll my hips and find the angle that sends her over the edge. She trembles from head to toe, her pussy pulses about my cock. Not wanting to hold back any longer, I drive myself into her until I come, my hips pumping on their own as I feel euphoria wash over me. We lay on the table, our bodies still joined, my cock throbbing inside her, for several minutes before I pull the pajama top down over her face.

"So was the edging worth it?" I ask.

She looks at me in a daze. "I guess..."

"How was the orgasm?"

She gives me a small smile. "Eleven out of ten."

"In other words, worth it."

With a little reluctance, she nods.

"No pain, no gain," I state.

"I don't know that I'd want to do it all the time, though."

I withdraw from her before the condom slides off. "As the sub, it's not your choice."

She wrinkles her brow. "Okay, but I haven't

agreed to be your sub."

I consider reminding her that the way she agreed to pay for her trip to Phuket is by spending a night at the BDSM side of my club, but I've got to finalize her commitment to Phuket first.

I flash her a grin. "You will."

She raises a brow. "Arrogant, much?"

"You know how many women—and guys—would leap at the chance to be my sub?"

"Doesn't matter. I've got to make my own decisions."

I toss the condom into a wastebasket and run a hand over her leg. "You know, I could just leave you tied to my table until you agree."

She blanches.

"Dining with a view," I consider aloud.

"Ha, ha, very funny," she derides. "You can untie me now."

"What's the magic word?"

"Please."

"And?"

She thinks for a second. "Sir."

I untie the pant leg from the chair. She sits up and shakes her head. "You are such a..."

"A what?"

She looks at me, mystified, probably wondering what she's doing with a guy like me. I could ask the same thing about her.

"I don't know," she finally replies, "but I feel a little less regretful that I threw soda in your face."

I decide to wipe the impish smile from her face with a smothering kiss. That comment will cost her. Leaving her wrists still tied, I throw her over my shoulder and carry her into the bedroom. After dropping her on the bed, I wind the other pant leg to the headboard.

"What are you—" she starts.

Grabbing her panties, I use them to tie her ankles together. Over at my dresser, I pull out a massage wand. She balks at seeing it.

"You don't have one of these?" I ask.

She shakes her head.

"They're basically a vibrator, only you can use this to relax muscles as well."

"Is that what *you* use it for?" she asks.

"Some of the time."

She scrunches her face. "So you've used it on other women before."

"I clean all my toys after each use."

I sit beside her on the bed, turn on the wand, and nestle it between her thighs. She yelps and twists away.

"You've had experience with a vibrator before," I state for confirmation.

"I live with three other women, and those things are noisy."

"So you only masturbate by hand?"

She nods.

"Then this'll be a treat," I say, holding down her hip and replacing the wand against her.

She squeals. "That tickles!"

Under my bed are leather restraints already secured to the frame. Turning off the wand, I reach under to grab one to clamp around her ankle after I pull off her panties.

"Hey! What are you doing?" she demands.

"Giving you an aid to help you hold still," I answer as I pull out the second leg restraint.

"This really necessary?"

"No. But it's fun."

After the second restraint is secured to her other ankle, I get off the bed and survey her, spread-eagle with her legs pulled to opposite corners of the bed, her arms tied to the center of the headboard. I drink in her nakedness except for the pajama top, which is bunched below her breasts. She looks awesome.

This is going to be fun.

I hop back onto the bed next to her and turn the wand back on. "Let's review how you're going to get yourself to Phuket. Are you going to get someone to cover you at the library?"

"Yes!" she cries as I press the wand against her vulva.

I pull the wand away. "And what about your internship?"

"I'm going to see if I can work remotely."

"What about your classes?"

"I'll get notes where I can. Maybe talk to the graduate assistant to see how I can make up

91

missed classes."

"Very good."

I move the wand back against her. With a half laugh, half cry, she squirms like a fish out of water. I'm amazed. This can't be her first time with a vibrator. I don't even have it on high.

"P-Please!" she gasps. "I need a break."

I grant her a short break. "Relax. Enjoy it."

She looks up at me with wide, doubtful eyes, but when I ask if she's ready, she draws a breath and nods. I return the wand between her thighs.

"Oh my God," she says through gritted teeth, still flailing and tugging against her restraints.

I could be an asshole and turn the vibrations higher, but I let her adjust first. Pressing down on her hip, I hold her in place so that she gets the whole head of the wand. Her back arches and her toes curl.

"Oh my God, oh my God," she repeats.

"Look at me," I order. I'm not going to miss out on seeing her face when she orgasms.

She turns her head slightly. Tension and helplessness are written across her. Her mouth opens wider, her eyes start to close. Her cries become more high pitched. And then she erupts, quaking beneath my hand, yanking uncontrollably at her bonds. When her climax is over and the vibrations prove too sensitive, she starts huffing and tries to squirm away from the wand. I turn it off and set it aside. My cock is rock hard and ready to go.

Grabbing another condom, I put it on and release one of the leg restraints. I twist her lower body to the side and push the freed leg up so I can access her pussy. This time, I sink my entire length in one go. She grunts. I close my eyes to savor how sweet it feels before lifting my hips back up.

"You like the wand?" I ask her as I piston my hips up and down.

"Yes."

"If you're good, I'll let you use it again. You want that?"

"Um, okay."

My pelvis slaps against the bottom of her ass and the back of her thighs. I like this angle of penetration. I like that I get to see her face and the flutter of her lashes, the way her eyes roll toward the back of her head when I hit the right spots. There's not much she can do but take my thrusting. After a while, I decide to change up the position. Time to take her from behind.

Reaching over, I release the other leg restraint, flip her onto her stomach, and elevate her ass by pulling a few pillows under her. Straddled over her calves, I aim my cock and sink in. I wonder what it would feel like taking her other hole, and if she's a virgin there. The question boils my balls. I drill into her, one long, forceful thrust at a time.

"I bet you've been told before what a great ass you have," I remark as I grope a buttock.

She's too busy grunting and groaning to answer. Putting a hand on her lower back, I vary the tempo and force, sometimes short and fast, sometimes deep and slow. The bed creaks with each smack of my pelvis into her ass. She cries out as I shove harder. But I know what will undo her.

Pausing my motions, I reach a hand around to play with a breast. Her pussy flexes around my cock and she pushes her ass back at me, seeking a return to the action. I give her nipple a tweak before reaching for her clit.

"Oh...my...God," she moans.

I start thrusting again.

"Ask to come," I remind her.

"Can I come?" she mumbles against the bed sheets.

"Yes, you can."

A few minutes later, shudders rack her body. As she comes, I plunge into her fast and furious till my climax bowls into me. For a moment, I might be fucking her harder than she can take, but I'm too blinded by pleasure and need to hold back. When the last of my body's tension drains out, I withdraw and lie on my back beside her. After collecting my breath, I free her wrists.

"Did I fuck you too hard?" I ask.

She replaces the pillows. "A little."

"Did you like it?"

She thinks for a second. "Maybe."

I smile and pull her to me. Who would have

thought? This opinionated choirgirl is taking to my kind of sex. The possibilities with Bridget could be endless...

CHAPTER TWELVE

BRIDGET
Past

I wake up in the middle of the night and remember the food never got put away, but Darren tells me to forget it and promptly pulls me back into bed. Within minutes, we're at it again, this time in a spooning position, which I've never done before. I love it because he strokes my clit while he bucks his hips into my backside.

He doesn't thrust into me as hard as last time, possibly because he doesn't have the same leverage lying on his side. I'm starting to feel a little raw from all the sex, but the orgasms are so worth it. Even as a horny teenager, I haven't been turned on like this. And even the quasi-BDSM elements are titillating. I didn't think they would be. The "sir" part of it isn't my favorite. Like there isn't enough misogyny and inequity between the sexes outside the bedroom.

But for now, I'll humor him. Because deep down,

I don't think he's a chauvinist, though I don't have any proof of that fact. Does being into the power play of BDSM automatically make him a chauvinist? Maybe. I really don't know enough about BDSM to say. If he confines the playing to the bedroom, then maybe not. So a male dominant, female submissive thing in BDSM isn't automatically rooted in chauvinism. It depends on the individual.

This is the kind of discussion I can see happening in a college seminar. I tell my brain to shut up so I can drift back to sleep in Darren's arms. He pulls a bedsheet over our lower bodies, and I tell myself not to get too caught up in all the feel-good hormones that have flooded me. It's too easy to fall in love with how great it feels to have the heat of his body embracing mine. I feel like Amy's fallen hard for JD, slacking off on school and her job as a waitress at a high-end restaurant. I don't want that to be me.

And somehow I've agreed to go to Phuket.

Crap.

Well, he can't hold me to it if I my supervisor's not okay with it.

"Something on your mind?" Darren asks.

Sunlight peaks in from between the blinds. I realize I've been staring up at the ceiling since waking.

"Thinking about Phuket," I reply. I turn to face him. "What would you do if you were in my position?"

He's lying on his back and puts a hand behind his head. "What do you mean?"

"Like, would you have lied and called in sick?"

"I'd just go."

"Yeah, but, let's say you really liked your internship and your supervisor isn't keen on you going. Would you lie then?"

"Maybe."

I already had a feeling he wasn't an angelic Boy Scout, but I'm a little concerned how far off he is. I remember him saying he didn't have a moral compass, but I thought he was just being facetious. "So you don't have a problem with lying?"

He glances briefly at me. "Depends on the situation."

"Like calling in sick to work when you're not sick."

"If I wanted to go to Phuket more than I wanted the job, then I'd go to Phuket."

"But that's not the hypothetical. The hypothetical is that you want the job more than you want Phuket."

"Fine. If lying means I get to keep my job and go to Phuket, then I'd lie."

I wrinkle my nose. It's not the answer I would have preferred to hear from him. "Your guilty conscience would let you do that?"

He gives a wry laugh. "Who says I'd have a guilty conscience?"

"Would you ever have a problem with lying?"

"Maybe, maybe not. Everyone lies. Unless you're some saint. Even then, I bet there's a lie in that history somewhere."

"There are degrees to lying."

"What's the biggest lie you ever told?"

I think back. "When my grandma asked who ate two of the Christmas cookies she had baked for her boss, I lied and said it wasn't me."

Darren lifts a brow. "And how old were you then?"

"Eight."

He groans. "You haven't lied since you were eight?"

"White lies, sure. I can't remember feeling as bad as I did about those cookies, though. I was sure Santa wasn't going to come that year."

"But he did."

"Yes."

"See. Lies aren't so bad."

"What was your biggest lie?"

His face darkens, and he doesn't answer right away. Not a good sign.

"There's too many to choose from," he growls, looking away.

At least he's honest.

"Just choose one," I say, feeling a little nervous.

He thinks for several beats, then says, "When I was in high school, I covered for JD and told the principal that JD was with me and therefore couldn't have been the one to put a stink bomb in the PE teacher's office."

Okay, that's not too bad a lie.

"Was JD the one who did it?" I ask.

"Yep."

"But that's not the worst lie you ever told," I venture.

Before I know it, he's on top of me. I can feel his super-hard cock against me.

"It's not," he acknowledges, "'cause I'm not as good as you, Miss I-don't-drink-before-I'm-twenty-one. You probably shouldn't be fucking a guy who lies and breaks rules."

He pushes the pajama top over my breast and takes a nipple into his mouth.

I gasp. "Yeah, probably not."

"I think you're trying to spice up your life, Bridge. Maybe being good is getting a little boring for you."

"I don't think being good is boring."

He presses his groin against me. I gasp because he's really close to entering me. Part of me actually wants it, and when his gaze locks with mine, I think he sees my desire.

"It'd feel good, Bridge," he says.

"What would?" I return, even though I'm pretty sure I know what he's referring to.

"Being inside you without anything."

I can barely catch my breath. "But I'm not on birth control."

"Nothing? No pill or…?"

"Nada. The pill gave me nausea, and I just haven't gotten around to trying anything else. Besides, pills or shots don't protect against STDs."

I breathe a sigh of relief that my responsible side has come through. That it even wavered makes me nervous. I'm beginning to think Darren might be a bad influence on me.

"All right," he says. "Why don't you play with yourself while I get the condom."

"Play with myself?"

"Yeah. Show me how you masturbate."

Okay. I slide my hand between my thighs.

"Bend your knees and spread your legs so I can see better," he directs as he reaches for the drawer of his bedside table.

I do so and tease my clit with a finger. He tears open the wrapper of the condom and rolls it down his shaft.

"That all you do?" he asks.

"Mostly. I share a room with Amy, you know."

He grins. "She ever catch you?"

I shake my head. "Though I walked in on her and her ex once."

Darren takes my free hand and places it over a breast. "Work it."

I feel myself up, feeling a touch self-conscious, but then, seeing the smolder in his eyes, I start to get into it.

"Nice," he says. "Keep going."

While I fondle and grope myself, he reaches for additional restraints near the ends of the headboard. I try not to think about how many women he might have bound to his bed.

Lifting my ankle, he claps on a restraint and does the same to the other. My legs are pulled apart in the air, toward the headboard behind me, making me wish I were more flexible. He pulls two pillows beneath me to elevate my butt.

"Don't stop," he tells me when I pull my hand from my clit.

He kneels before me and sinks his fingers into my slit. I continue to masturbate while he finger-fucks me. Our fingers graze against each other sometime. I can feel my wetness flow down to my crack. After several minutes, I'm on my way up to the peak of rapture.

I groan with delight when he replaces his fingers with his cock. Its hardness is exactly what I need. He rolls his hips at first, filling me with pleasure. Then he thrusts harder. I grunt in surprise.

"Too hard?" he asks.

"No," I answer.

He bucks harder. "Can you take that?"

I nod.

But the next set of shoves are definitely uncomfortable. I grimace.

"Too hard," he replies for me.

"Yeah."

He reaches for the wand that was left in the bed

and turns it on. "Hold this to your clit."

Oh no. The wand is fabulous, but it takes a little getting used to at first. I touch it tentatively to my clit and try not to laugh. He returns to rolling his hips more gently. I press the wand a little longer on my clit this time. He watches me, amused and turned on. When it seems his patience is done, he grabs my hand and presses the wand more fully on my clit.

"Ahhh!" I cry out.

But my body adjusts to the vibrations and welcomes the stimulation. Darren moves his hips faster and harder, shoving me toward the headboard. He increases the pounding as the delicious percolation between my thighs intensifies. Soon, Darren is driving into me like there's no tomorrow, but the stabbing pain is overshadowed by my impending climax.

"Oh, fuck!" I swear before I explode, my legs straining wildly against the restraints.

Darren grunts his way to his climax, but my body is too busy being buffeted between waves of euphoria to notice. When I'm finally able to pull away the wand, the area between my thighs is throbbing like crazy. Little tremors still shoot through my legs haphazardly.

"You can keep the wand," Darren says when we've both recovered from our orgasms. "Practice with the higher settings."

My eyes glaze over. Higher settings?

"Then let me know how it goes."

"I've got to report back to you?" I joke.

"Yes," he replies before undoing the restraints from my ankles.

"You're serious."

He looks at me like I'm weird for thinking otherwise.

"And if I don't fit in any of this 'practice?'" I challenge.

"Then there are consequences."

"Consequences? Like what?"

He gives me a devilish grin. "You're welcome to find out."

I look at the wand. I get the feeling this "gift" will prove to be a Trojan horse.

CHAPTER THIRTEEN

DARREN
Past

"**C**an you believe fucking Manny Wu?" JD asks me through my speakerphone as I drive back to the city after dropping Bridget off at her apartment. It took all of me not to grab her and throw her in the backseat for a quickie before she left, but there's a lot she feels she needs to accomplish before Phuket.

"Wants me to help him with his massage parlors, but he's not fronting any money," JD continues. "Not a fucking dime."

"What's wrong with you getting a percentage?" I ask.

"Like I'd trust the Park Street Boyz to give me the right cut. Manny swears they're legit, but that's Manny's problem: he believes shit too easily. Man, he would not shut the fuck up last night. Luckily, Amy was in the restroom most of the time and too drunk to understand what was going on when she got back. I finally told him flat out I'm not doing anything for him. You know what he said?"

"No," I reply, my mind half on the homework assignment I had given Bridget, to work up to the middle setting on the wand.

"He asked me, 'Why the fuck not?' So I told him the truth. That he's a loser. He's struck out too many times in the past, he doesn't even belong in the Rookie league."

"Poor Manny."

"Someone's got to tell him the truth. Why you gotta feel bad for Manny, anyway? The guy's pathetic. Oh, speaking of pathetic, my sister shared an updated guest list and Joseph Mok is coming. Guess he and the groom roomed together at USC."

Mok and I had a run-in years ago when I was hanging out with Tony Lee at a bar in Vietnam. I had started hitting on a woman I didn't know was with Mok because she had seemed receptive of my attentions. Mok took offense. He kept glaring at me through the night as he drank beer after beer. I had one too many drinks as well, so when Mok and his friend came up to me and Tony, I didn't even attempt diplomacy. Not sure I would have even if I wasn't intoxicated.

I ended up with a black eye, just before I broke Mok's nose. All four of us were hauled into jail, though Tony's brother got us out earlier so I had the chance to flipMok off as I left. The next day, I happened to come across Mok's woman walking out of a tea shop and ended up sleeping with her. Not sure if Mok ever found out, and I don't give a shit if he did or didn't.

"I don't have a problem with him as long as he stays out of my way," I say. "By the way, you get your sister a wedding gift yet?"

"I still got time. What did you get her?"

"Cheryl put together a little Hawaiian vacation package."

"Shit. I got to get someone like Cheryl working for me. It's not like my sister needs anything from me, though. Her boring-ass husband can buy whatever they need."

Andrea, JD's sister, is marrying an entrepreneur who recently sold his start-up to a Fortune 100 company for nine figures.

"How long you plan on staying in Phuket?" JD asks.

"Maybe ten days, though I'm not sure Bridge can stay that long."

"Will you listen to yourself? What should it matter how long she can stay?"

"She's got a job and an internship. She wasn't sure she could go in the first place."

"What is the matter with her? Doesn't she know you could have invited a hundred different women to go instead?"

"That wouldn't matter to her."

I can hear JD shaking his head. "You picked a doozy. Her pussy must be something special."

Oh, it is.

As I pass through the toll booth and onto the Bay Bridge, it starts to rain. The forecast for the week is wet and cold, but I'll be in warm, sunny Thailand soon enough.

Earlier, I had taken a photo of Bridget on my phone and sent it off to Cheryl for the passport. I had expected Bridget to protest that she didn't look her best, but after she had washed her face and brushed her hair, she was ready to go. Kimberly would have taken at least half an hour to do her makeup and another half an hour to do her hair.

Later that day, I text Bridget to see if she had tried the wand I gave her. She replied that she was working on a paper for her health policy class. I asked if she had gotten anyone to cover her shifts at the library. She hadn't. I told her she had better try or I would come over and apply the wand to her myself.

An hour later, she texted that she'd found someone to cover at least one of her shifts.

I tell her to call me when she's ready to use the wand.

After spending some time going over the trip to Thailand with Cheryl, I wander over to the BDSM side of the club. I watch a dominatrix peg her sub while he licks the pussy of another woman. I wonder again if Bridget has ever had anal sex. I don't have a good sense of her overall experience with all things sex. She had mentioned a boyfriend once. Some football player. Sounded like they had dated a while, but they were younger at the time. Bridget's *still* young. She can't even legally drink yet. I haven't dated anyone in college since I was in college myself.

Deciding the scenes are turning me on too much, I go back to the regular side of The Lotus where I'm approached by Tommy, a longtime family friend, to hold a suitcase for Old Dog, a known assassin. I'm guessing the suitcase contains cash, but, per my usual M.O., I don't ask.

"You're the only one I trust to turn this over to," Tommy tells me. "You're dependable, just like your dad. The triad should have you take over for your dad. I get that you were in school at the time, but that job should be yours now. You've a right to it. I keep telling the Vanguard that the guy they have heading up counterfeiting right now just isn't as good."

"I've been approached by Lee Hao Young about it," I reveal as I place the suitcase in a safety vault in my office and have one of my security guards stand watch.

"About damn time! That's great!"

"I haven't said yes yet."

Tommy does a double-take. "Why not?"

"It's the last thing my mother would want me to do."

"Look, I like your mother, but women get scared easily. It's part of their genetics, and she's right to want to protect her only son. But what happened to your father was a fluke. I'll talk to her. Let her know you'd have a lot of people, like myself, looking out for you."

My mother likes and respects Tommy.

"You were meant for bigger things than this club," Tommy adds.

I cock my head at him. "You know my mother. She rarely changes her mind."

"Yeah, I know. Sharon is the most stubborn person I've ever met. But, ultimately, you don't need her approval."

"I know that."

I think back to the nights I heard her sobbing in her room after my father died. I didn't want to go back to UCLA at the time, but I did it mostly for her. My father had wanted me to get a college degree, too. Not because it would help me with the triad but because, in stereotypical Chinese style, he regarded it as a badge of honor. And I shied away from getting too involved in the *Jing San* business because of her. But it has been several years since my father died, and I'm getting bored with The Lotus. I'm ready for a new challenge, and my father would have wanted me to continue his legacy.

"Besides, you want to make your father proud, right?" asks Tommy.

I let out a breath and find myself wishing Bridget was coming to the club tonight. "Yeah," I answer.

Tommy claps me on the back. "Maybe you'll

make an even bigger mark on the *Jing San* than your old man. Then all you need is a wife and kids."

I must have balked, because he laughs. "I know, I know. You're still young. Enjoy the women while you can."

I raise a brow. "*You're* married. That hasn't stopped you."

"True. Your dad was strangely devoted to your mother, but you could be more like me instead."

Tommy chuckles at his own statement before taking his leave.

I walk up the stairs to my balcony and find JD on a call.

"Fuck! Another one?" he curses into his phone. "What do you expect me to do about it? Shit! We'll just have to take it as a loss."

JD kicks the coffee table after hanging up.

"*Baijiu?*" I offer.

"Shit, yeah," JD responds.

I wave to one of my servers.

JD flops down on a lounge chair and, throwing his head back, rubs his eyes.

"Amy coming tonight?" I ask.

"Later. She has to work tonight at the restaurant. Says she's missed too many shifts lately."

I consider seeing if Bridget would come with her friend, but I want Bridget to get her work done so she has no excuses for not going to Phuket.

JD pulls out his cigarette case.

"You know the rules," I tell him.

"It's just one smoke."

"I don't want to get busted on some small shit."

"Yeah, you're right. Like how they got Al Capone on taxes."

"I've got marijuana if you want that."

"Hell, yeah."

After the server delivers the *baijiu,* I tell her to get JD some weed.

JD downs a shot of *baijiu,* then another.

"You pound too much of that with the weed, you're not going to be able to get it up for Amy," I warn.

"Yeah, yeah. You getting any tonight? You want Amy to bring Bridget with her?"

"I don't need to pound pussy every single night."

"If you can, why not?"

"Bridget has to finish a paper for class."

"You're lucky; you can just walk over to the other side of your club to get booty."

It's true. I could. But I'm more interested in finding out how Bridget gets on with the wand.

A mutual friend, Alejandro, comes up to the balcony to jaw with us and smoke some pot. Amy arrives about the time the two of them are too stoned to hold a real conversation. JD offers her a joint, which she accepts.

"Aren't you going to say anything about my outfit?" Amy asks. "I just got it today."

With his eyes glazed over, JD looks over her strappy top and leopard-print skirt. "Hella sexy.

Right, Alejandro?"

Alejandro nods. "Name's Alejandro. What's yours, *chica*?"

"Amy."

He jerks his head toward JD. "You're not with that loser, are you?"

She giggles. "Actually, I am."

"Sorry to hear that." Alejandro rolls his head to me. "You got anyone for tonight?"

I shake my head.

"You can have me," Alejandro jokes.

"Sure, but I only pitch," I reply.

He pours himself a shot of *baijiu*. "Ah, you're no fun."

Being a cheap date, Amy doesn't take long to get high. Knowing that Marshall or someone else from the security team will keep an eye on JD, I head upstairs to my residence and video call Bridget.

"How's the paper coming?" I ask after casting the video call onto the flat-screen TV above the fireplace. I sit down on the sofa.

"Pretty good," she replies. Her hair is in a ponytail and she wears a Cal hoodie.

"How long you been working on it?"

"Since dinner. Hey, you think you could get me the recipe for that rice and mango dessert? I'd love to make it for my roommates."

"Sure. But you got to use the wand first."

She purses her lips. "I share a room."

"Not at the moment. Amy's here at the club."

113

"Already?"

"Yep."

"I thought she'd stop by here first."

"So I think it's time for a wand break."

She hesitates.

"Where's the wand?" I ask.

Her cheeks turn color. I love the way she blushes.

"In the closet," she answers.

"Get it."

After a brief pause, she goes to close her bedroom door first, then retrieves the box with the wand.

I put my arms over the back of the sofa and settle into the leather upholstery. "What are you wearing besides a hoodie?"

"Baggy sweats."

Not the sexiest thing but functional for my purposes.

"Take the wand out and put it in your sweats," I instruct.

"You want me to do all this in front of you? I thought I was going to report back to you after I was done using it."

"You missed your window."

She glares at me. "I wasn't aware I had a time limit."

"Now you know. Like I said, you can do it. Or you can wait for me to come over and jam that thing between your legs for you."

114

Now she scowls. I try not to laugh.

She grabs the wand from the box.

"Move your phone so I can see," I tell her.

She pauses. "You're not recording this or anything?"

"No. Recording shit isn't my thing. I like my sex live—preferably in person."

Satisfied, she holds her camera in one hand while she nestles the wand in her sweats with the other.

"Nice," I praise. "Now turn it on."

She turns it onto the lowest setting, then whimpers as the wand hums quietly in her sweats.

"Put the phone back so I can see your face," I say.

Seeing the helpless pout on her features makes my cock stretch. I adjust myself. "That feel good?"

After a long pause, she answers, "Yes."

"Are you leaving it in place or moving it around?"

"In place."

"How fast do you think it would take you to come?"

Her brow furrows. "I don't know."

"Where do the vibrations feel best? On your clit? Your pussy lips?"

"Um, everywhere."

"You want to try the next setting?"

She shakes her head.

"Try the next setting," I direct.

She looks as if she's struggling against something.

"Bridge, try the next setting. Don't make me ask twice."

"Okay. Just..."

She takes a moment, braces herself, and increases the setting. Her mouth immediately drops open. I know she wouldn't try to trick me. Plus, I can hear the faster, louder vibration.

"Oh my God," she says through gritted teeth.

"Hang on. Don't come just yet."

She shakes her head and squints her eyes.

"You always have to ask first."

But she has no time. With a cry, she starts to spasm. The phone clatters to the floor. I hear her soft wail, and then light panting. No longer pressed against her flesh, the wand sounds louder. A moment later, it's turned off.

Heat swirls in my loins as I imagine her pussy pulsing from the climax. After a minute or so, she collects herself and picks up the phone.

"What just happened?" I ask.

"I came," she replies weakly.

"Was it a good one?"

She nods.

I smile. "Good."

I decide not to point out that she didn't ask to come, which entails a punishment in my book. I'll save that for when she's back over at my place.

CHAPTER FOURTEEN

BRIDGET
Past

*L*ast night, I managed to work on my paper a little more after using the wand for Darren. And since Amy was probably spending the night at JD's place, leaving me the room to myself, I actually used the wand before going to bed. The orgasms don't engage my whole body the way sex with Darren does, but they still feel great, and they come fast. Usually it takes me twenty or more minutes to masturbate myself to the end. The wand cuts that time in quarters, and the orgasms are stronger.

The next day, I think through what I would say to my internship supervisor, Linda Rosen. I can't believe I'm actually asking for time off to go to Thailand. It's crazy. I don't do this kind of stuff. To make sure I haven't lost a screw, I call Coretta, a woman I trust second only to my grandmother.

"So there *is* a man in your life," Coretta says. "I

thought I sensed something."

I'm sure I didn't say anything during my last call with Coretta that would suggest that I'm seeing anyone, but maybe she has a sixth sense.

"He a student at Cal, too?" Coretta asks.

"He's actually a few years older," I answer as I sit before my desk with one foot on my chair. "He went to UCLA."

"By a 'few years older,' how many are we talking about?"

"I'm guessing five."

"That's a little more than a 'few,'" Coretta teases.

"Maybe four."

"And what does he do?"

"He owns a club in the city."

"How'd you meet?"

I tell her the story of how Darren and I first met and how I ended up throwing my drink in his face.

"Well, your grandmother probably wouldn't have approved of throwing drinks at people," Coretta commented, "but it sounds like this young man deserved it."

"He admits he did."

"Good. So how did he win you over?"

I think for several seconds. "He let me teach him how to boil an egg."

"You're telling me he doesn't know how to boil an egg?"

"Actually, I don't know a lot of guys who know

how to boil an egg. I bet the majority of guys in college don't know."

"You might be right about that. Especially in your generation."

"And Darren has a unique excuse for not knowing. His meals are made for him by his chef."

"Goodness. Are you saying he's rich?"

"He's not like anyone I would ever think to find myself dating. He's a businessman, he *is* rich. Born that way, I'm assuming, because he grew up in Atherton. We are so unalike, really. And not just because we're on different ends of the socioeconomic scale."

"There's truth to 'opposites attract.'"

"I guess. It feels strange and right at the same time. But I really don't know him well enough. And then he invites me to Phuket, Thailand—"

"To where now?"

"Thailand."

"Your guy invited you to Thailand. The country Thailand?"

I laugh. "When he first said Phuket, I thought he was referring to a restaurant."

Coretta is quiet. "That's a far place to go."

"I know. My roommate, Amy, is dating his cousin, and she was invited, too. I mean, maybe flying off to Thailand is no big deal for them, but it is to me."

"Your mother would be jealous."

"And I am *not* my mother."

"Going to Thailand doesn't make you your mother."

"I know. And unlike my mom, I have responsibilities that I take seriously. Class and work. Darren insisted I could work it out, and he's right that I probably could. But *should* I even try?"

"Hmmm. How badly do you want to go to Thailand? And can you trust this guy?"

That's the key question. And what does it say about me if I go?

"I think so," I answer. "But how well can you know a guy after just a few weeks?"

"He must be head over heels for you to be asking you to Thailand."

"You'd think, but that's not the sense I get from him."

"Then why'd he invite you to Thailand?"

"Because he wants company, and he's interested in me at the moment."

"What does your gut say?"

"That I can trust him, but it doesn't seem reasonable to fly halfway 'round the world with someone I barely know. What do you think Grandma would say?"

"Well, she might feel like I do, which is a little nervous since I don't know the guy, but she'd also be happy that you have the opportunity to experience a trip to Thailand. He's paying, right?"

"Yeah. No way I can afford to go otherwise."

"Your gut ever steer you wrong?"

I ponder the question. "Not really."

"And you said your roommate's going, too?"

"She's very excited."

"And her family's letting her go?"

"I think she's going regardless. Would you go?"

"Well, the farthest I've ever traveled is Florida. Still, my life is complete, with or without a trip to Thailand. But it *is* exciting. Like winning a big prize on a game show."

"I'm not going to mourn the opportunity if I don't go," I consider aloud. "Who knows, this may not be my only opportunity to go."

After talking with Coretta, I'm a little less sure about Thailand. I decide that if Linda doesn't go for it, I won't go.

But Linda, a woman in her early fifties with tight curly hair and librarian glasses, is enthusiastic. "Who is this guy?"

"The cousin of a guy my roommate's dating," I reply as I run documents through the scanner.

Linda sits down at my computer. "What's his name? Where does he live?"

"Darren Lee. San Francisco"

She types both into Facebook. "Is this him?"

I look at the photo of a Caucasian man. "Darren's Asian. He runs a nightclub, The Lotus."

"This isn't him," Linda murmurs, looking at the profile pic of an older Asian man. "Your guy has a Facebook account, right?"

I shrug.

"Oh, wait, your generation is more on Instagram or Snapchat, right?" Linda asks as she types in "The Lotus" and "San Francisco."

No direct results. There's a restaurant by the same name, but it's not in the city.

"How can a business not show up? Is it brand-new?" Linda asks.

"It's been around a few years."

Linda searches Yelp but finds nothing. She does a broad internet search for Darren Lee and The Lotus, then Darren Lee and San Francisco, and The Lotus and San Francisco.

"It's like your guy and this club don't exist," Linda murmurs.

I look over her shoulder. "Try UCLA. That's his alma mater."

The search turns up his name in a list of graduates for the Economics Department four years ago but not much else.

I have an idea and pull up Instagram on my phone. I type in Kimberly Park. Sure enough, she has an Instagram account chock-full of selfies showing off her amazing body. Scrolling through her account, I find a photo of her and Darren.

"That's him with his ex-girlfriend," I say, showing my phone to Linda.

Linda pulls her glasses down her nose to see the photo better. "Oh, wow, he's hot. You've got to go to Thailand."

"But we have grant applications to work on," I

reply.

"A trip to Thailand. A super-sexy guy. What more do you want? In fact, with a guy like that, it wouldn't matter where we went. If he wanted to hang out at a quarry, I'd say, 'hell, yes.'"

"I could work on the applications remotely as long as there's internet access," I say.

"I know I said I wanted to find the funds for our food recovery vans as soon as possible, but an extra week is not going to make a huge difference. You should go."

Linda was my out if I decided against going. After Linda and her assistant leave for the day, I stay behind, trying to get as much done as possible. A little after six, I get a call from Darren.

"Where are you?" he asks.

"Working at my internship in Oakland," I answer.

"You had dinner?"

"Not yet."

"Are you in downtown Oakland?"

"Near Lake Merritt."

"I'll pick you up in twenty then."

He just assumes I'll have dinner with him? That I don't have somewhere to be?

Truth is, I was just going to head back to Berkeley and read through some case studies for my health policy class or work on a problem set for statistics. And I have to have dinner at some point.

So I say okay and give him the address before

hanging up. When I walk out of the office building later, I see him and his Porsche waiting for me. He looks devastatingly sexy in his leather jacket and form-fitting jeans.

"That's a familiar outfit," he remarks of my black jeans, boots, and sweater.

I smile. "I'll wear it often, just for you."

He opens the passenger door for me. "What do you feel like for dinner?"

I think for a moment. "Soul food. How about Maybelle's?"

He plugs Maybelle's into the GPS. "So you work it out yet with your internship about going to Phuket?"

"Yes."

"Great. You're all set then."

I hesitate.

"What's the matter?" he asks.

I turn my body to face him. "I'd like to go, but I want to pay my fair share."

He raises an eyebrow. "How well does your job shelving library books pay?"

"That's just it. I can't really afford this trip."

"And I told you I've got this."

"But you shouldn't have to."

"Look, the villa is paid for. It doesn't cost extra to have you there. If you want to pay for your meals, fine."

"There's the plane ticket."

"That'll probably set you back about 20K."

"What?!"

"I booked a suite. It's an international flight."

Turning back around, I sink into the car seat and stare out the front window. Holy crap. That's more than a year's tuition.

I let out a breath. "Okay, that is way too much to be paying for. I don't need a suite. I'm perfectly fine flying coach."

He narrows his eyes at me. "You're not flying in one end of the plane while I'm in another."

I calculate in my head, "On a payment plan of a hundred dollars a month, it would take me almost four years to pay you back."

"You're not serious."

"I am. I can't let you treat me to a twenty-thousand-dollar flight."

"Why the hell not?"

"That's more than some men spend on their fiancées."

"It's all relative. It wouldn't bother me taking a woman I met off the street to Thailand."

I'm not sure how that makes me feel, though I think he means to reassure me.

"Anyway, I'm not that type of woman," I say.

"What type of woman?" he returns, sounding a little exasperated.

"The kind that likes to be wined and dined by some sugar daddy."

"I told you how you can pay me back."

My cheeks grow warm. I had forgotten about

that. "So you want me to prostitute myself for the trip."

"*You're* the one who wants to pay me back."

I try to remember exactly how we had left it. "You wanted *one* night at your club?"

"I said one, but I'm up for more."

I shift in my seat. "For twenty thousand dollars, I probably owe you more than just one night."

He grins. "You said it, not me. I won't argue with you on that."

I sigh.

He shakes his head. "Why is this so fucking hard for you?"

"Because I don't get invited to Thailand. Ever. And the most I've ever paid for a plane ticket is three hundred dollars for round-trip economy with change fees and no refunds."

"You said you would make Phuket work."

I cross my arms and avoid his gaze. "That was said under duress and in the heat of the moment."

"So you'll say anything during sex?"

My blush deepens. *No. That doesn't happen. Only with you.*

"I guess we could do a combination of the BDSM club and a payment plan," I murmur.

He pulls the car into a parking spot and turns off the engine. Unbuckling, he turns and grasps my jaw, forcing me to look at him. "You're going to Thailand. My way. And you're going to enjoy it. No more of this payment shit or I'll spank you right here in the car."

He's serious. I shouldn't let him get away with

making threats like that. And yet...it sounds kind of sexy when he says it. Already I feel a warm tingles in my body.

I am in so much trouble.

CHAPTER FIFTEEN

DARREN
Past

I can't believe Bridget. Aside from my mother, I've never had to work so hard to convince a woman of anything. It's crazy that I'm even involved with a woman like this, crazy that I want to fuck her brains out this much.

At first, she doesn't respond to what I've just said, like her breath is caught in her throat. Her skin feels soft beneath my fingers, and I hold off on kissing her because I'm curious to hear what she has to say to the spanking.

It seems desire sparkles in her eyes, and when she speaks, her breath is ragged.

"You're threatening me," she states. "You ever heard of the phrase 'you catch more flies with honey?'"

I envision her lying naked upon a table, honey dripping off her body.

"We can do that, too," I murmur as I pass my

thumb across her bottom lip.

"I just—I don't want you to get the wrong impression about me," she tries.

"What's the 'wrong impression?'"

"That I'm some gold-digger who can be bought by fancy trips to Thailand."

I stare into her eyes intently. "You're the opposite of a gold-digger—and that's not any better."

She's taken aback. "How's that?"

"You going to Thailand with me should be an easy, done deal. Think of it as a gift of a lifetime. Like you won the lotto or something. Accept it and appreciate it."

"I *do* appreciate it."

"Do you? Then why are you making it such a big deal?"

She looks hurt. Her lashes flutter. "I..."

"The money doesn't mean shit to me, okay? Frankly, I don't care if you *are* a gold-digger. I just want to be able to fuck you when I want, how I want, as hard as I want."

With that, I finally smother her mouth with mine. If she had something to say, I don't care anymore.

I dig into her mouth, pushing my tongue against hers, consuming what I can. She starts kissing back, which turns me on even more. Grabbing the back of her head, I manipulate her so I can take her at different angles. I kiss her harder, longer, deeper. Till she's breathless.

"You know you came without permission yesterday," I murmur over her lips.

"What?"

"With the wand last night, you didn't ask to come."

"Was I supposed to?"

"I said you always have to ask before you come."

She furrows her brow, possibly in disagreement.

"You don't remember me saying that?" I inquire.

"You did," she acknowledges.

"So what do you want your punishment to be?"

"Seriously?"

"I don't mess around when it comes to my rules."

Her shoulders sag. To add to her difficulty, I kiss my way from her lips, along her jaw, and to her ear, which I nibble and tug with my teeth.

"I don't know," she moans. "I've never had to ask to come before."

"You're going to get yourself nice and wet. And then you're going to blow me. And that barely qualifies as a punishment."

She appears okay with that.

"Take your jeans off," I order.

"There are people walking by!" she protests.

"It's dark and the windows are tinted," I reply.

She looks out the car to see that no one is near before undoing the button and pulling down the zipper. She shimmies the garment down her legs. When she pulls them off, she shivers. I turn the car heater on.

"Now the underwear," I say next.

Once she's naked from the waist down, I pull aside her left thigh and reach for her pussy. It's already damp. I slide my fingers over the flesh, grazing the bud hiding between the folds.

"Make yourself wetter."

She spreads her legs farther and caresses the area between. I undo my own jeans, which, luckily, are button-fly so I don't have to worry about my cock getting scratched by the zipper. Pulling out my hardened cock, I stroke the shaft while watching her.

"Now taste yourself."

She hesitates but then lifts her fingers to her lips.

"That's it," I encourage. My cock pulses when she pushes her fingers into her mouth. "You look so naughty and sexy right now. You knew you were this naughty?"

She shakes her head.

"Go back to playing with yourself."

With one hand, she spreads her pussy lips so that her other hand has better access to her clit. My cock is rock hard now.

I put my hand on the back of her head to guide her to my cock.

"Do you have a condom first?" she asks.

"In the glove compartment," I answer.

She opens it and finds the condoms. After

opening one, she rolls the condom over my shaft. I would have preferred head without the rubber. In fact, I can't remember ever having a condom on when receiving a blow job.

"I don't want to wear a condom next time," I tell her.

"You can get tested," she said, grasping my cock. It flexes in her hold. "There's a clinic in Berkeley that's open until ten o'clock."

I'm there.

I push Bridget's head down over my cock. She takes me into my mouth. I groan in satisfaction. She sucks on my cock, and the pressure is amazing. That clinic better produce fast results. If this is how good it feels with a condom, I can barely wait to go without one.

I lift my hips to push my length deeper into her mouth. Fisting my hand in her hair, I guide her rhythm.

Fuck. Yes.

I tighten my grasp, tugging on her hair, and push her down farther. She gags, so I relax my hold. When she recovers, I return to the previous motions, making her go up and down my cock. Once in a while, when she goes as far as she can, I hold her in place and try to get her to take a little more. She usually starts to choke. I let up and allow her to dictate her own speed and depth.

Reaching for her ass, I give her a light spank, then grab and shake a buttock. I find her slit and sink two fingers inside. She mews into my groin.

In a bona fide punishment, I'd blow my load and let her stew in her arousal, making her wait hours, maybe days to come. But I want to be buried inside her.

I pull her off by her hair and move my seat back. "Get on top of me."

When she doesn't move over, I grab her. She yelps as she bumps into the stick shift. I settle her over my lap, wind my hand through her hair and tug on it before bringing her lips back to mine. As we engage in a mini-marathon of kissing, I unbutton her sweater, then reach up her shirt to unclasp her front-close bra. Pushing aside the bra cups, I grope a breast, kneading it, digging my fingers into the pliant flesh. She moans softly against me. I grasp her hips and grind her against me. My cock thrills to the pressure. It wants more.

Lifting my hips, I spear myself into her.

It feels fucking marvelous every time.

Sex in the front seat isn't the most comfortable, but I like how her breasts are right in my face. I push up her top and assault a breast. With a moan, she starts to roll her hips at me.

"Put your feet up on my thighs so you can get more leverage," I tell her. She complies and is able to push herself all the way up my cock. "Nice."

I go back to licking and sucking on her nipples. Taking her hands, I make her feel herself up, my hands atop hers. I want to see her come, see if she remembers to ask before doing so.

I pin her arms to the steering wheel and buck into her fast and hard. In this position, her head is pushed up against the top of my car. I watch her breasts quiver with my thrusting, her brows knit and her mouth drop open.

"Oh, sh...oh, geez," she grunts.

"Ask to come," I remind her.

"Can I c-come?"

"Yes, but next time there are no more reminders. Got it?"

"Y-Yes."

"Now thank me for letting you come. Usually I'm not such a nice guy."

"Th-thank you."

I slow the action and roll my hips more leisurely before I go back to pounding her. I'm going to fuck the I'm-too-good-to-accept-a-trip-to-Thailand out of her.

With a gasp, she erupts, spasming on my cock. It's followed by a cry. If I wasn't holding her to the steering wheel, her body might be jerking all over the place. I pull her mouth down to mine before she's done climaxing and pump my hips several times to drive the tension in my groin out of my cock. My erection throbs madly inside of her.

Wrapping her arms around my neck, she slumps against me. I lie there till my breath returns to normal. Holding onto the condom, I ease out of her and notice the windows are fogged up.

"We should get dinner so that we can make it to this clinic," I say.

She makes it back to the passenger seat. "I'm really hungry now."

After we're presentable again, we head into the restaurant. It's a hole-in-the-wall type of place but cozy with character.

After the server takes our orders, I sit back in my chair and observe Bridget. She still has that post-coital glow. Though her hair is a little mussed, she looks beautiful.

"So I don't want to hear any more about the cost of the trip or excuses not to go," I tell her.

"They're legitimate reasons. I mean, if you were in my shoes, would you go halfway around the world with a man you haven't known for a long time?"

"What do you need to know?"

She stares at me. "That I can trust you."

I shift in discomfort but retort, "What's the worst that can happen?"

She sighs. "I don't know. You sell me into the sex trade there?"

I don't say anything because that kind of shit does happen. It almost happened to Tony's friend, and I know a few names associated with porn using kidnapped women.

"I'm joking," she says.

"I know that."

"You just looked really serious all of a sudden."

"What do you want from me? Some kind of guarantee? Insurance?"

"Insurance would be good. Or some kind of collateral."

I think for a moment. "How about ten thousand dollars?"

"What?"

"I'll put ten thousand dollars into an account for you. You can name your beneficiary. If anything happens to you, they get ten thousand dollars."

"You would do that?"

I must be going crazy. The amount of money doesn't bother me, it's the hoops I'm jumping through just to ease her mind.

"Don't make me have second thoughts."

She purses her lips in thought. "My beneficiary only gets the money if there's proof I'm dead. What if I'm just missing?"

"Look, your friend Amy's going. Your internship knows you're going. I assume your other roommates would know, too. If anything happens to you, I'll be the first suspect."

"True. Okay, you can keep your collateral."

Jesus fucking Christ.

"You're going to Phuket then," I say. "End of story."

"End of story. Which means no spanking."

I lean across the table toward her. "That's what you think."

CHAPTER SIXTEEN

BRIDGET
Past

A spanking doesn't scare me. I've got padding where I need it. But I'm not going to go out of my way to get a spanking.

After dinner, Darren drives us to the clinic where we both get swabbed for STDs. The results take a few days.

"No sex without protection, no drinking before twenty-one," Darren says as he drives me back to my apartment. "You're the straightest arrow I've ever met."

I keep coming back to opposites attract, which I didn't really believe in before. Darren claims he doesn't have a moral compass, but he hasn't shown me he *doesn't* have one, even if it may not be a large one.

"Hanging out with you might have a corrupting influence on me," I joke.

"I hope so," he replies.

"Or maybe the opposite will prove true."

"God, I hope not."

"What's so bad about being good?"

"It doesn't fit my lifestyle."

"How come?"

He stares ahead at the road. "It just doesn't."

"You worried that you won't attract as many women without your bad boy image?" I tease.

"No, I don't worry about that, even though it's true that women prefer bad over good."

"I don't think that's true."

"No? Then how come all your favorite heartthrobs in movies, shows and books are billionaire playboys?"

"They're not *my* favorite."

He turns to stare at me. "Then what are you doing with me? Why aren't you with some guy who's out there saving the environment or registering voters and shit like that?"

What *am* I doing with a guy like Darren?

I cross my arms. "I don't know. Lapse in judgment, I guess. And the sex is good."

My answer surprises him at first, then he smiles broadly. "Works for me."

"And what's a bad boy like you doing with someone like me?" I challenge.

"The sex is good."

"But it's not like you can't get it with one of the models wandering around your club. I'm guessing pussy is pussy for a guy."

"You said it, not me."

"Seriously. Why are you hanging out with me?"

"Lapse in judgment," he replies, his tone a little dark.

I think he means it.

"So we have that in common, along with the sex," I summarize.

"That's good enough for me."

I guess it's good enough for me, too. At least for the time being, though I'm a little disappointed he doesn't see more than that. I'm not expecting a long-term serious relationship with Darren. But is he capable of any level of commitment?

"Just so we're clear," I say, "an STD test doesn't do much if we're looking to have sex with more than one person at a time."

"You looking to have sex with someone else?"

"No! But I don't think I'm the concern here. It's a typical gender inequity: men are less likely to be monogamous."

He looks disgruntled, probably because he's a typical guy who doesn't like discussions pertaining to relationship status.

"I'm not looking to have sex with anyone else at the moment," he grumbles.

"Okay. Just let me know if that changes. I'd let you know if it changes for me."

The thought seems to startle him. "When you're with me, there's no one else unless I allow it."

"As long as that rule goes both ways."

He opens his mouth as if he's about to protest but changes his mind. He pulls up in front of my apartment building.

"You don't have to park," I tell him. As usual in Berkeley, parking spots are hard to come by. "I hope I didn't make you uncomfortable. I know how much guys love to talk about relationships."

"What relationship? I thought we were just having sex."

"I still like to be clear what's on or off the table."

"I'd like to put birth control on the table."

Given how often Darren and I are having sex, it would be smart to have something more reliable than condoms.

"I'll look into it," I reply.

He looks at me with hunger. "Good. I'm looking forward to fucking you without a condom."

I swallow with difficulty. The thought turns me on, too.

"And before you go to bed tonight, I want you to text me your measurements," he says.

"Why?"

"You need an outfit for the wedding."

"How do you know I don't already have one?"

He lifts a brow.

"I could borrow something from Simone," I tell him.

"There's no discussion on this—unless you want to do it splayed across my lap."

"I can go shopping on my own."

"Did you hear me, Bridge?"

I bite my tongue—for now.

"Measurements," he reiterates. "By midnight."

This trip to Phuket is turning into one of the most complicated situations for me. I can hear Darren's response: It wouldn't be so complicated if you didn't *make* it so complicated.

Back in my apartment, I try to forget about Phuket and Darren and review the steps Taiwan took to successfully contain Covid-19 for my health policy class. I text Darren my measurements and let him know to keep the outfit under seventy-eight dollars, the balance in my bank account. Maybe I can try to squeeze in another shift at the library before I leave for Thailand. I should have insisted on getting my own outfit for the wedding. I don't know how or why I let him have the last word. Maybe I need to assert myself more so I don't end up on some slippery slope with him, and the next thing I know, he's dictating my life.

At least I got him to take the STD screen. I half expected him to balk, and I'm glad he didn't even complain. *See, you're not all bad*, I could have said to him.

But there is something off about him. I don't know why I think that. The bigger mystery is why

I'm going to Thailand with him if I feel that way. Is it because I like the sex that much?

Must be.

I figure sex can only take us so far, so when he gets bored of me and wants to go back to dating models or I come to my senses, we'll move on to our normal lives. Until then, I'll just enjoy the chemistry and rush I get in his company.

The following day, I manage to get a same-day appointment at the student health center to look into birth control shots. Luckily, I'm still in the 7-day window from my period so the shot can take effect immediately.

The next few days, I don't see or hear much from Darren except an update that my passport and travel visa are ready and to check in about the STD results, which are clean. I credit him with knowing that I need to focus on my schoolwork and internship. Which is more than I can say for Amy, who wants to talk about Thailand every possible minute. She's shown me over a dozen outfits, returned nearly as many, and gone shopping at least three times. I end up bringing my laptop to the library just so I can have some peace and quiet.

"Do you think I should go with the matching tropical bottom for this bikini or the solid black?" Amy asks, holding up the options, after I get back from the library late Thursday night.

"They both work well," I say. "How was work today?"

"Oh, I quit. They weren't happy with me taking a week or more off since I had missed a few days already. I think I'm going to go with the solid black. Or maybe I should bring both. Yeah, I'll bring both. You going over to The Lotus tonight?"

I shake my head. "My paper for health policy is due tomorrow."

"I should probably skip it, too, though JD said he'd be there. I don't want him to think I don't have a life outside of him."

I'm tempted to say she doesn't seem to think about anything else, but I keep my mouth shut. Instead, I say, "So things are going well between you two?"

"OMG, it's *amazing*. He's definitely *the one*. I think he feels it, too, otherwise why would he invite me to his sister's wedding? I mean, I'm going to be meeting his family. I can't wait for my family to meet him. They're going to be so impressed. I check off all the boxes with JD: he's Asian, he went to a good school, he's a successful businessman. He's sexy as hell. The sexy part is my box, of course."

"Your parents aren't going to be disappointed he's not a doctor?" I tease.

Amy smiles. "Given how much money JD must make, I think they'll live with it."

"He imports chemicals?" I recall.

"Something like that. It's kind of boring."

She grows quiet.

"Something the matter?" I ask.

143

"Just that he seems stressed from work lately. My Cantonese is a little rusty, but it sounds like a recent shipment isn't going well, and he might lose out on a lot of money. Maybe I should go over to The Lotus tonight in case he needs cheering up."

While Amy gets ready to go to the club, I get a call from Darren about coming over to view the outfits Cheryl will have picked out for me. The flight's on Sunday, so there's not a lot of time left.

"Maybe tomorrow," I reply. "I need to finish my health policy paper, which is due tomorrow, and I'd like to finish at least one grant application."

Secretly, I also want to find a way out of this outfit business.

"How's the paper coming along?" he asks.

"Pretty good. I'm just having second thoughts about my conclusion."

"What's your conclusion?"

"That, had the US done a fraction of what Taiwan did, we could have saved hundreds of thousands of lives."

"You don't really believe that?"

"There's always the issue of scaling up. Taiwan's population is a small fraction of the US's."

"We're the richest country in the world. Why should that stop us?"

"It shouldn't."

"We're supposed to be badass, right?"

"That's a compelling argument. The United States can replicate Taiwan's success on a larger scale because we're 'badass.'"

"Don't we have the resources?"

"We should. Our GDP is much larger. In fact," I plug some numbers into calculator app, "our per capita GDP is fifteen percent higher. I could argue that the US has more issues to deal with, but ultimately it's a matter of prioritizing what's more important. Okay, I feel better about my conclusion. Thanks."

"So I'll pick you up tomorrow at nine."

After hanging up, I sit down on the bed. I'm proud of myself for the amount of work I finished this week, even though thoughts of Darren crept into my mind often. I called Coretta to let her know I was going to Thailand. She asked me to check in with her daily. I assured her I would. Coretta always treated me as if I were one of her own.

"You want to come with me to the club tonight?" Amy asks as she applies another coat of mascara.

It's tempting, but I shake my head. "I told Darren I'd come over tomorrow."

"I still can't believe we're going to Phuket. In just a few days!"

I flop down onto my pillow and stare at the ceiling. I can't believe it, either. Phuket. Thailand. And all I have to cover is meals?

Just then, I remember the one payment Darren would accept: a night at the BDSM side of his club.

Am I really up for that?

CHAPTER SEVENTEEN

DARREN

Past

Bridget looks horrified.

I seriously don't get this woman at all.

Standing in the middle of the living room, she stares at all the outfits Cheryl had laid out. Cheryl has good taste, and I was sure there would be something in the collection that Bridget would take to. Instead, she eyes the clothing as if they're bugs instead of designer fashions.

"These don't look like they cost seventy-eight dollars," Bridget says sternly.

I cross my arms over my chest. "Like I was going to take your money. It was my idea to get you clothes for the trip. I'm taking care of this."

Bridget does a double take. "You mentioned an outfit for the wedding. One outfit."

"So what are you going to wear the rest of the time?"

For a second, she's speechless. "You got a whole wardrobe?"

"How can you not like clothes? All women like clothes."

"Sure, but that doesn't mean I want a whole new wardrobe!"

I guess I shouldn't be surprised by her reaction. This is the woman who couldn't deal with accepting a free trip to Thailand. But I thought clothing would be a different story.

"An *expensive* wardrobe," she adds, spotting a price tag.

I rub my temple. "It's not that much more than the airline ticket. I told Cheryl to shop the cheap places for you."

Bridget's eyes widen. "Her definition of 'cheap' is wildly different from mine."

"Fine, you can do the shopping."

"I'll take care of getting an outfit for the wedding, but I'm not going to buy an entire wardrobe."

"I'm offering you a shopping spree. Isn't shopping a woman's favorite pastime?"

She rolls her eyes. "That's an old-fashioned stereotype."

"Yeah? I dare you to ask ten women whether they love to shop or not. The only one saying no would be you."

"I have clothes."

"You're not going to walk around Phuket wearing sweats. For one, you'd be too hot. It's summer there."

"I have shorts. Are you embarrassed by what I'm going to wear? That's it, isn't it? I'd bring down your image, just like my ugly sweater didn't mesh with your swanky club."

I let out a frustrated breath through my nose. I can't believe we're having this argument. For a relationship built on sex, Bridget is more effort than I bargained for. "I said we're not having a discussion about this," I say.

"You didn't mention anything about clothes. I can't pay for this, and I can't accept his. *That's* the end of the discussion."

I stare at her in disbelief. I want to wring her neck. Or…

Stepping toward her, I grab her and pull her facedown onto my lap while I sweep the shoes Cheryl bought off the coffee table.

"What—are you—"

She struggles against me while I hold her down by the neck and yank her leggings down past her ass.

"This is not the way to get me to change my mind!" she huffs.

"I know that. This is just for fun," I snap before groping a buttock.

"This is assault."

149

I almost tell her I've been guilty of worse. I smack my hand to an ass cheek. The sound is amazing. She yelps and starts to struggle harder. I spank her a few more times before sliding my hand between her thighs.

She stills.

My blood pumps faster. This is the test. I might have crossed a line with Bridget, but I haven't had a woman not give in before, sexually or otherwise.

"That's not going to get me to change my mind, either," she mutters as I fondle her clit.

Right now, I don't give a fuck about the clothes. I give her ass a hard wallop.

"Geez!" she cries out.

I spank her until her ass is a nice shade of red, then go back to playing with her clit. She goes from grunting to groaning. Now that she's not struggling as much, I fist my other hand in her hair and pull her head up, forcing her to crane her neck and arch her back. I agitate my digits faster against her flesh.

"Oh my God," she murmurs.

After I get her wetness flowing, I go back to spanking her. I haven't given her a safety word, but she hasn't asked me to stop, either. I rub a buttock and sink my fingers into it. This is a nice piece of ass. I can't wait to see how cane marks look on it.

"Your ass was made for spanking," I remark, grabbing an orb, then slapping it. "You know that, Bridge?"

When she doesn't answer, I yank on her hair. "I asked a question."

"I thought it was rhetorical," she grunts. "I did not know."

I admire the hue. "It's looking so pretty for me right now. You ever been fucked in the ass?"

"No."

Something to work towards. I plunge my middle finger into her wet, hot pussy and imagine what it would feel like being in her virginal asshole. Withdrawing, I add my forefinger before pushing back in. She moans.

Last time, I said I wasn't going to remind her to ask to come. Let's see how well she remembers.

"Oh my God," she whimpers as I alternate my hand right-side up, then upside down.

Curling my fingers inside her, I find her preferred spot and angle. After slowly stroking her, I increase the speed of my thrusting.

"I'm going to…" she starts. "Can I come?"

I don't answer but tighten my grip on her hair.

"Can I come, sir?"

She's even more trainable than the German Shepherd I had growing up.

"Yeah, come," I reward her.

She comes undone over my lap with long groans and sustained quaking and the occasional shudder when I jab my fingers back inside her. She lets out a haggard breath.

I flip her onto the oversized ottoman and push her knees to her chest. Holding her ankles in one hand, I undo my pants with the other.

"What's the birth control situation?" I demand, pulling out my throbbing erection.

"It's, um, good."

Perfect. I aim my cock at her slit. In this position, it would be so easy to sink into that other hole. It looks so cute and puckered.

"Grab your legs," I tell her.

She obeys. I brace an arm against the ottoman and push into her wet heat.

It. Feels. So. Fucking. Good.

I knew it would. The wetness against my skin, the feel of flesh against flesh. Pleasure shoots up my spine and boils in my balls. With a groan, I pull my hips away from her before sliding my cock back in, burying myself as far as I can go. I still myself to savor every inch, letting my cock throb inside of her.

"That feel good?" I ask her.

Her eyes appear extra bright as she nods. As I take my time rolling my hips, I keep my gaze on her face so that I can catch every furrow, strain, pout or grimace. After a while, I push her legs down and to the side so that her body forms an L-shape, only she's still on her back. She moans as my cock strokes a different part of her pussy.

"You like that?" I ask.

"Yes."

"You want to come like this?"

"Yes, please."

I accelerate my thrusting. Her lashes flutter quickly. Her brows knit together. She grabs the edges of the ottoman behind her head.

"You like your spanking?" I ask.

"Uh..."

I shove myself hard into her.

"Yes!"

"That the truth?"

She bites down on her lower lip and nods. I pound into her more intensely.

"Oh, geez...I'm gonna come!"

"Not yet."

"I can't—"

"I said not yet."

She squeezes her eyes shut and appears to do her best to hold back her orgasm. "I..."

Her body starts to jerk beneath me. She emits a sobbing groan. It sends me over the edge. With a few furious thrusts, I hit my peak. Grunting loudly, I empty my cum into her while pleasure shakes me from head to toe. When the last of the shudders has left my body, I press my forehead to hers.

"Coming without permission," I tell her. "You know what the punishment will be."

"More spanking?" she guesses.

"You go to Thailand. My way. On everything. Absolutely zero discussion. And, yes, more spanking."

CHAPTER EIGHTEEN

DARREN
Past

"*H*oly shit," Amy gasps as we step into the suite of the aircraft after walking down a dedicated jet bridge.

A flight attendant introduces himself as Lim and asks if we would like Dom Perignon.

"Hell, yeah," Amy answers, even though she already had two glasses back at the private lounge where we dined on steak with foie gras and fried quail egg.

After we settle into leather seats with our champagne and Bridget's first ever Iced Milo, the rest of the crew introduce themselves. I can tell Bridget feels awkward. Maybe it's because she's wearing clothes that she didn't buy and is being addresses as "Ms. Moore" by the flight staff. At least she doesn't look out of place in the leggings and off-shoulder sweater that Cheryl bought her.

"This feels...surreal," she murmurs. "I don't feel like myself."

"You're going to enjoy the ride," I remind her.

She nods. "Where's Cheryl?"

"Taking a flight tomorrow. She wanted to finalize tax stuff for our accountant before leaving."

"*This* is the way to fly," Amy gushes as she videos our surroundings.

"You a member of the Mile High Club?" JD asks her as he props his feet up on a footstool.

She giggles. "No. Airplane bathrooms are gross."

JD grins. "Then you get to join the club in style today. Though it might by kinky fun to slum it in a lavatory in coach."

Amy wrinkles her nose. "They're so small. And they smell."

Lim returns to offer a copy of every newspaper they have onboard, such as the *Wall Street Journal* or *New York Times*.

JD waves him away and turns back to Amy, "So what's the worse place you've ever had sex?"

Amy thinks. "I don't know. In high school, my senior year, my ex and I did it in his bedroom one day, but his younger sister's bedroom was right next to his. She was fourteen, but it was still kind of awkward thinking she might have heard us."

I look at Bridget. "What about you?"

"I briefly dated a guy who roomed with two other guys in a dorm. They had beer cans, junk food and their underwear all over the place."

"Your turn," JD says to me.

"Outdoor bathroom at a gas station off Highway 5," I answer.

"Ewww," Amy groans. "That's worse than an airplane lavatory."

I look at JD and wonder if he's going to tell the truth about the worse place he had sex: a brothel in Vietnam where stray dogs wandered in and out of the room.

"A garden bench," JD says. "The thing was old and made of wood. I must've ended up with a dozen splinters in my ass."

Amy giggles. "So where's the best place you ever had sex?"

"Wherever you are, babe."

Amy looks like she's going to melt.

After the plane has taken off and reached cruising altitude, Lim offers us another drink and takes our meal orders. Bridget looks over the menu and asks about a tea, which Lim describes in detail about cherry blossoms and red fruits wrapped in hand-sewn teabags.

"Five courses!" Bridget exclaims as she looks over course selections. "We just ate back at the lounge. I don't even know what some of this stuff is."

"I can order for you," I offer, curious how much control she'd cede.

"I'll figure it out," she replies, eventually choosing the fennel salad with mizuna, chicken and mutton satay, a noodle soup, Boston lobster, and a peach cake inspired by Chanel. "I'm going to feel guilty eating all this."

"You want us to move down to coach so you can feel less guilty?" I ask.

"No. I wouldn't make you do that. Besides, I don't know that you'd survive fifteen plus hours in coach."

"Cute."

"I mean it. You ever flown coach before?"

"No."

JD pipes in. "You couldn't pay me to fly coach."

"That's how most of the world flies—if they can afford to fly in the first place," Bridget says.

"Not my fault the world is comprised of the have and have-nots."

"Yeah, you couldn't make it past ten minutes in coach," I tell him.

"Maybe you should try it," Bridget suggests. "Makes you appreciate all of this so much more."

"I don't need to fly coach to appreciate this."

Bridget turns to me. "How about you? Want to give coach a try? Just for a little bit?"

I stare at her. She's joking, right?

"At least slum it in business class," JD advises.

Bridget grabs my hand. "Come on. You're going to see how those of us in the lower classes live."

Lim comes over to see if we need anything. Bridget asks if there are any empty seats in coach. He doesn't comprehend what she's asking.

Referring to me, Bridget says, "He's never flown coach before."

"Okay," Lim says, still with a puzzled look on his face as he goes to check on her request.

I turn to Bridget. "You realize that it costs about a thousand dollars per hour to fly in the suites?"

"We won't be in coach for that long."

Lim returns and informs us there are several empty seats. Bridget chooses two towards the back of the plane.

"I'll let the attendants in coach know you're coming," Lim says. "If you need anything, they can call me."

"We won't need anything," Bridget assures him.

"What about your supper?"

"We'll have it when we get back."

She drags me downstairs and through a partition to where the seats must be made for skinny people with short legs.

Bridget smiles at me. "You can have the middle seat."

I sit down next to a scruffy-looking man asleep against the window. He smells as if he hasn't taken a shower in weeks. In front of me sits a man at least three hundred pounds. I don't know how he fits in his seat. He chooses to lean his seat back, squishing into my knees.

Bridget chuckles. "Want my seat instead?"

She sits next to the aisle but I notice a kid sitting behind her, and he's walking his feet on the back of her seat. His mother is busy trying to keep the toddler on her other side quiet.

"I'm good," I reply.

An attendant goes through asking for our drink order.

"I don't think they serve Dom Perignon here," Bridget tells me.

I decline a beverage while Bridget tells me she'll have cranberry juice. It arrives in a plastic cup with a tiny bag of pretzels.

The man beside me shifts, sending a new wave of body odor toward me. He starts to snore loudly. The toddler behind him shrieks. The sound rings in my ears for seconds after.

"Happy?" I ask Bridget.

"I never considered myself sadistic," Bridget says, "but it's kind of funny seeing you suffer."

"Ha, ha. You are paying for this."

Her grin drops into a frown. "All right, we'll go back. You lasted all of twenty minutes. I just need to use the bathroom before we head back."

I'm about to tell her that she's better off holding it and using the bathroom in the suites when I decide to follow her instead. The lavatory is located next to where the drinks and snacks are stored and where the attendants sit, but the attendants are still distributing beverages to the folks sitting in the front rows.

"Hey!" Bridget exclaims when I grab the door to keep it from closing behind her. "What are you doing?"

"Getting the full coach experience," I reply wryly. I can barely close the door with the two of us inside.

"You're not—"

"Your idea to come down to coach."

I check that the lid is down on the toilet before turning her around to face the wall. I wrap an arm around her and kiss her neck.

"What if there's a line of people needing to use the bathroom?" she asks with alarm.

"There's more than one lavatory in coach, right?"

"What if they hear…stuff?"

"I can be quiet," I say before lightly sucking on her neck.

I put my other hand at her crotch and start to rub.

"I do not need to join the Mile High Club," she protests, but I heard the telltale hitch in her breath.

"Too bad. It can be fun."

I rub her harder through her leggings. She whimpers. I lower myself to press my hard-on against her ass.

"This might top my list of worst places to have

sex," she hisses.

"We'll make it a quickie then. Get it over with faster."

I turn her head so that I can access her mouth. I notice she kisses back. My hand goes back to caressing between her legs. After I've worked her up through her clothes, I pull her leggings and panties down past her ass. I then take my cock out and rub the tip along her folds. She braces her arms against the walls of the lavatory.

"I can't believe we're doing this," she murmurs.

"Shhh," I return and press my cock into her wet heat.

She groans. I bury myself as far as I can and start a gentle bucking, watching as my cock disappears and reappears beneath her ass. She gasps loudly when I thrust too hard. I clap my hand over her mouth. Gradually, I build up speed. I try to keep my pelvis from slapping into her ass to minimize the noise. The angle of penetration seems to work for her. She grunts in earnest. Her body strains toward her climax.

"You realize you've got to be super naughty to let a guy fuck you in an airplane," I growl as I quicken my pumping.

I can see her eyes widen in the mirror.

"Such fucking naughty pussy," I grunt as I send her over the edge.

As her body shakes, her arms slip from the walls. I catch her, shove myself deep and reach my

162

own orgasm. The release feels incredible. I don't think I'll ever get tired of spilling my seed into her.

Afterwards, Bridget quickly wipes herself and pulls up her underwear and leggings.

She checks herself in the mirror. "I hope we weren't too long or too loud."

"Too late now," I respond.

She opens the door and steps out. I follow her. An attendant is throwing used cups into the trash and looks surprised to see both of us emerging from the bathroom. Even without seeing Bridget's face, I know she's blushing hard. Bridget quickly walks down the aisle, heading back to our section of the plane.

"Anytime you want to go back to coach…" I start to say as we head upstairs.

She scowls at me.

Supper is waiting for us. Bridget seems to have worked up an appetite from her membership activities and digs in.

After supper, she and Amy walk about the plane. A few others are flying in the suites as well: an haute couture fashion designer, a corporate executive, and an MLB player and his wife.

JD and I lounge in the sitting area. I hear Amy coo over the amenity kits by Yves St. Laurent and the pajamas and slippers by Givenchy.

JD overhears it, too. "Isn't it cute how impressed they get over this shit? I feel sorry for guys who can't afford to impress their women."

"You don't feel sorry for shit," I say.

"Yeah, you're right. Sucks to be them."

JD puts on a Bose headset and listens to music. I get a text from Tommy:

> Talked with your mom. She chewed me out a new one.

I text back:

> What did you expect?

JD, reading over my shoulder, asks, "Tommy know that you got approached by Lee Hao Young?"

I stare at my cousin. Even though Amy and Bridget seem too engaged to pay attention to us, we shouldn't be talking triad business in a place like this. JD has gotten looser with his talk lately.

"We can talk later," I tell him with my gaze on Amy and Bridget returning. "And you should be more careful. You never know who can hear."

"Yeah, yeah."

The tone of his response doesn't inspire me with a lot of confidence. One of these days he might run his mouth off at the wrong place, at the wrong time.

CHAPTER NINETEEN

BRIDGET
Past

I couldn't have dreamed up a more luxurious flight. The mattress on the double bed in our suite was comfier than my own bed, and the crew had sprinkled rose petals over it and included another bottle of champagne.

As soon as Darren and I were snuggled under the covers, his hands were in my pajama pants.

"What if these sliding doors aren't that soundproof?" I ask. "Plus, the attendants seem to check up on us every five minutes."

"The Do Not Disturb light is lit," Darren replies. "And if you're really worried about sound, give me your panties."

"What?"

"Give me your panties."

I give him a dubious look but shimmy out of my pajama bottoms and underwear. I hand the stretch-ace boyshorts to him.

He opens my mouth and stuffs my panties in. I make a protesting sound.

"Shh. You're worried the crew might hear," he reminds me.

I glare at him, but I'm soon distracted by his hand caressing me between the legs. My body is such a sucker for his touch. It's distressing, really. And it seems to be getting worse with time. Before I know it, I'll be committing armed robbery for him.

After he's got me all hot and bothered, we go from missionary position sex to reverse cowgirl. My mouth gets dry from the panties, and there's another problem with having my mouth stuffed with underwear.

Darren pulls me prone on top of him, my back to his chest, his cock still buried in me. "You can't ask to come, can you?"

He swirls his fingers in my pubic hair before sliding lower to find my clit. I whimper as he strokes the engorged bud, made slippery by my wetness.

"Please, may I come?" I inquire, but the words come out a muffled mess.

His free hand plays with a breast while he masturbates me. "What's that, Bridge?"

You know damn well what I'm asking.

But I try again.

"What would you rather have: the chance the crew might hear us or the chance to ask permission to come?"

I groan at him. But his fondling feels so good, I don't want him to stop. I'll come without asking. What's he going to do? Make me go shopping? I won't do it.

His fingers wreak havoc on me, like they always do. He gives my nipple a harsh pinch, and seconds later, I'm jerking and bucking against him. Holding me to him, he shoves his hips into me. He can't seem to get the penetration he wants, so he rolls me beneath him. He pulls a pillow beneath my hips and is able to go deeper. After pounding into me forcefully, he roars, his legs trembling beside mine. I feel a stream of heat filling me.

Breathing heavily, he lays down beside me. "So what do you want your punishment to be for not asking to come?"

I pull my panties from my mouth. "That wasn't fair."

"Who says I'm fair?"

"I *did* ask!"

"I didn't hear it. I just heard a bunch of mumbling."

I grab the pillow and hit him across the chest with it. He grabs my wrists and, rolling on top of me, pins my hands to the bed.

"Behave yourself, Bridge."

"I don't deserve to be punished and you know it."

"Don't worry. I'll make it good. Something you'll come to beg for."

He nuzzles my neck and kisses his way down to my belly. As he licks me between my thighs, I relent. It's getting to be a habit all too soon. A small warning bell rings in my gut, but it's soon drowned by the swelling of rapture.

*****

I manage to sleep six hours on the plane. After getting up and dressed—I opt for a simple sundress—we dine on a filet mignon with eggs breakfast, served with Jamaican Blue Mountain Coffee. We watch a movie with JD and Amy. I work on my statistics homework for about an hour. Not long after lunch, the flight begins its descent.

Looking out the airplane window, I'm blown away by the cerulean ocean water and the white sandy beaches.

Maybe it's because I've never been in another country, but I love Thailand. It's a balmy eighty-five degrees when we arrive in the early afternoon. I drink in everything from the airport to the ride to the resort and am so absorbed, I don't think to take photos.

Our driver names the different beaches we drive by and explains that the winter season tends to bring drier weather, calmer seas, and sunnier skies. Nothing but sunshine and temperatures in the eighties are expected for the next ten days.

Darren tells us the resort that we're going to

was developed by distant relatives in the Lee family and sits on what is effectively a private beach, which are not allowed in Thailand, but the Lee family purchased all the surrounding land.

"O.M.G.," whispers Amy when the car pulls up to a multilevel resort built into the side of a cliff and overlooking the ocean.

I don't even have words.

The driver says he'll have our bags taken directly to our villas. Following Darren and JD to the lobby, Amy and I try not to fall over our own feet as we ogle our surroundings.

"O.M.G.," Amy says again as we look down from the lobby at the huge infinity pool below. It almost looks like you can swim from the pool straight into the Andaman Sea.

After JD and Darren have checked in and a resort staff member has offered us drinks, another staff member asks if we wish to take the elevator or stairs down to the villas.

"Stairs," I answer so that we can see more.

"O.M.G., this is yummy," Amy says of her Singapore Sling.

We walk by huge lounging areas with incredible vistas. From the stairs, I can see tennis courts, another swimming pool, one of the three restaurants set in the middle of a pond, and a pavilion for spa treatments, with another for yoga. The staff member tells us the resort is one of the few with direct beach access, goes over the

169

amenities offered, and provides logistics such as the availability of internet and international plugs.

As if the main resort area wasn't astounding enough, the villas leave me speechless. JD and Darren each have their own one-bedroom villa with full kitchen and dining area. The large windows and glass doors make all the rooms extremely bright even with the shade of the surrounding trees, and each villa comes with its own private pool.

The king-size bed beneath a romantic canopy faces the beach. The balcony doors are open, allowing in a faint breeze.

"What's the matter?" Darren asks me.

"I...I just feel like the luckiest person in the world," I reply. I almost feel like crying. I wish my grandmother or Coretta were here. They deserve an extraordinary place like this after how hard they've worked.

Darren walks up to me and cups my face in both hands. His tone is slightly threatening. "Your job is to enjoy it all."

I nod. I want to thank him for picking me for this trip, but the words are caught in my throat. He brushes his lips over mine. The kiss deepens. My head, already swimming from taking in everything so far, drowns in awe.

"Now about your punishment..." he murmurs atop my lips.

A squeal surprises us apart. A slender young

woman with long, shiny black hair with bangs over thick-lashed eyes steps through the balcony doors.

"It's so good to see you!" she cries as she throws her arms around Darren.

Behind her follows a young man with a quiff cut, what look to be expensive shades, and a bronzed tan. He and Darren shake hands.

"Bridget, this is the bride and groom," Darren introduces. "Andrea and Preston."

I shake hands with the couple. They're friendly enough but don't seem that interested in me. I wonder if they think I just happen to be Darren's flavor of the month?

Andrea turns back to Darren. "I heard your mother might not make it, but tell her we're saving a seat anyway in case she can. Tomorrow's the rehearsal dinner, which you're of course welcome to attend. Just let Sarah, the wedding planner, know. And we'll probably go clubbing over in Patong tonight. That's the one drawback of this beach. Not as much nightlife."

"Where will the wedding take place?" I ask.

"On the beach. We decided to keep it small, with only two hundred guests. If you want to join us for dinner, we have reservations at seven."

After Andrea and Preston leave, Darren grabs me over to him and continues where we left off. But JD and Amy show up next.

"My dad's up in one of the cliffside villas," JD tells Darren. "Want to come with? He hasn't seen

171

you since your father…"

JD looks at me briefly, maybe thinking Darren hasn't told me about his father's passing, though I don't understand why that would be an issue regardless.

After the men are gone, Amy lays down on the bed and appears to do snow angels. "Can you believe this place?"

I sit down next to her and run my hand over the super-soft linen. "No, I can't."

"I don't think I can go back to Cal after this. Simone and Kat are going to be so jelly when they see the photos."

I go get my phone. "That reminds me, I promised Coretta I'd take lots of pics."

Amy sits up. "What do you think of Andrea?"

"She seems nice."

"Yeah. We didn't talk much, though."

"As the bride, she probably has a million and one things on her mind."

"Still, you'd think she'd take a stronger interest in her brother's girlfriend. She's really cute looking, just like JD. I wonder why he's not bringing me to meet his dad yet."

I shrug. "I'm sure you'll get to meet the dad soon enough. We're here for a week."

"Ten days for me and JD."

Darren is staying ten days as well, but a week was the most I was willing to stay. And I spoke with Cheryl—after thanking her for getting the

172

clothes—to have her change my flight back to economy class. Of the many outfits she had purchased, I'd selected only three plus a swimsuit to bring along. I packed some of my own clothes.

When the guys return, I ask if we can take a walk on the beach. JD declines, so Amy passes on the walk.

"Before we go on the walk," Darren says, "we still have to take care of your punishment."

"For what happened on the flight?" I ask.

"Yes."

"But…" I growl when I can see that he's not going to change his mind.

He digs through one of the bags, which the valet had placed in our villa earlier, and takes out a small black box. He opens it to reveal two shiny balls connected by a string looped at one end.

"You know what these are?" he asks.

"Ben Wa balls," I guess.

"You ever try them?"

"No, but I'm about to?"

I guess having to do some Kegel exercises isn't too bad a punishment.

Darren has me lie on the bed and lift up my dress. Pulling aside my underwear, he rubs one of the balls along my clit. When I'm nice and wet, he slips the ball inside me, then pushes the second one in. He tongues my clit, and I have second thoughts about going for a walk on the beach. The sensation of the balls plus the cunnilingus are a nice pairing.

And getting in an orgasm would be a nice start to the walk.

But Darren stops and pulls me off the bed. "Now we can check out the beach."

"With the balls inside?" I ask. "What if they fall out?"

"You have the lighter beginner balls. They shouldn't take that much work to keep in."

As I take a few steps, I'm not sure I agree. It's strange enough having something stuffed up my vagina that isn't a tampon.

At least the beach is practically deserted, which surprises me, given we're in tourist season, so I have privacy if I have an accident. For a while, all I can think of are the balls inside of me, but I do notice the softness of the sand is otherworldly. I feel like I'm stepping on baking flour.

"How are the balls doing?" Darren asks with a grin after we've walked quietly for a few minutes.

"Nice to see you're enjoying my torture," I retort.

The balls are a constant reminder of my arousal and the orgasm I was hoping to have before the walk. My body hasn't had the chance to settle down, and I don't know that it will with these damn balls in me.

"How do they make you feel?" he asks.

I look at him. The breeze tussles his hair. He looks sexy as ever in a button-down shirt, untucked with the sleeves rolled up, over khaki pants.

"Horny," I blurt.

He laughs.

I head to the water and dip my feet in to see if I can get my mind off the balls, but Darren pulls me to him and smothers my mouth with a heavy kiss. His hand encircles the back of my head, locking me in place, my mouth his to plunder. I love the way he kisses, even though I find it overwhelming at times. The agitation in my loins flares, accentuated by the balls.

He scoops me up in his arms and carries me to an area beneath a palm tree. He continues to take my mouth as he sets me down in the sand. I yelp when I feel him reaching up the skirt of my dress. I want to keep kissing him, but there's no guarantee that we're alone. We had walked by a couple sunbathing not too far from here. I push his hand away.

"You want to go back to our villa?" I inquire against his invading mouth.

"No," he mumbles.

I grab at his hand, which cups my mound, and try to wriggle from underneath him. "Darren, this is not a private beach."

"No one's going to access it."

"The hotel guests? We walked by a couple already."

"You said you were horny."

"I can wait till we get back to our villa. Can't you?" I dare him.

"Sure, but I don't want to."

I try to push him off me. "Our villa isn't even that far."

"Stop struggling. You're going to get sand in our clothes." He grabs my wrists and pins them to the ground. "Don't make your punishment worse."

"Ugh. Coming to Thailand with you has its drawbacks."

He palms a breast through my dress. "And its perks."

He bites at my nipple through the fabric and cups me between the thighs again. I debate which is worse: getting caught having sex in public or worsening my punishment. The latter involves a lot of unknowns, and there's chance we could get away with the first.

His hand slips into my panties and rubs my flesh. Now I don't think I have the will to do anything but the first option. I try to swallow my moans as he intensifies his fondling, which makes the balls inside me quiver. My body starts to writhe for a different reason.

When he undoes his pants, I look to see if anyone's around. He pulls aside my panties.

"Aren't you going to take the balls out?" I gasp when I feel his erection pressing against me.

For an answer, he sinks in several inches.

Holy crap.

I feel the balls being pushed deeper inside me. It's unlike anything I've felt before. He rolls his hips, pressing the balls farther each time. I feel as if my body is one long tuning fork. Each time he thrusts, I'm hit with vibrations of arousal from head to toe. I hope I come soon because as magnificent as the sensations are, they're almost too much to take.

"Oh...God," I groan, grabbing onto his shirt.

The balls hit areas that have never been touched before.

"Oh God, oh God," I pant.

He stares into my face expectantly, and I remember to ask, "Can I come?"

He grinds his hips to mine. "You're not worried about people anymore?"

I shake my head. He pauses to kiss my neck and shoulders. I clamp down on his cock and the balls.

"Please," I try.

"Maybe we should wait till we get back to the villa."

I glare at him. "You're such a..."

"Go on. Finish your sentence, then ask to come again."

"...tease. Can I come now?"

"That's not what you were going to say, was it?"

"No. Sir."

"Not a bad recovery attempt. Tell you what, I'll let you come if you agree to take an anal plug tonight."

I balk. I'm going to have more objects inside

me? And what exactly is an anal plug?

Darren resumes his thrusting, and my doubts evaporate.

"Okay," I agree.

"Okay, what?"

"I'll do the anal plug. Just let me come."

His cock stabs into me in quick, short bursts, shaking me and the balls inside me. My orgasm erupts, shattering me into pieces. I don't realize I've screamed aloud till Darren clamps his hand over my mouth. After some hard and deep shoving, he reaches his climax. I lay on the sand in disarray, little pulses still rippling through my veins.

Like Amy would say: O.M.G.

Darren pulls out, brushes the sand off his crotch area and zips his pants.

He gives me a hand up. I have sand in my hair, on my dress, on my butt and even in my underwear. I take a step and wobble because the balls are still in me.

"I can't wait to get these balls out," I mutter.

"What if I made you wear them the rest of the night?"

My eyes widen. "You can't *make* me."

He grasps my jaw. "Sure I can. And we're just getting started, Bridge."

CHAPTER TWENTY

DARREN
Past

After we return to the villa, I remove the balls for Bridget, order room service and take a dip in our pool with her. We join Andrea and Preston for dinner in a private area outside, overlooking the sea. Our party occupies two tables. There are four bridesmaids and groomsmen, plus the respective families of the bride and groom. I introduce Bridget to JD's father and JD's aunt, Elaine. JD's father is not much for socializing and merely grunts. Elaine, however, takes more of an interest in Bridget, but not because Elaine is friendly.

"She's so cute," Elaine says, taking the seat next to me and setting down her aperitif. "I didn't know you liked them so young."

Bridget, seated on my other side, can hear everything Elaine says.

"She is legal, isn't she?" Elaine asks

If I hadn't brought Bridget with me, I might have ended up sleeping with Elaine. She looks youthful for her age, but regularly wears more makeup than some people don for Halloween.

"I'm legal," Bridget answers for me.

I survey what's around Bridget that might get tossed in Elaine's direction.

Elaine smiles. "So where'd you guys meet? How long have you been together?"

"We met at my club," I answer, "and I haven't kept count."

"A few months? Half a year?"

"Less than that."

Elaine arches a dramatically teased brow. "And you've invited her to Andrea's wedding?"

"I think JD dared him to ask the first person he saw," Bridget jokes.

"That's so cute." Elaine twirls her fingers into the hair at the base of my neck and leans toward Bridget. "You're so lucky, you know. There's always a ton of women throwing themselves at Darren."

"I *am* lucky," Bridget says sincerely.

Elaine drops her hand from my head to my thigh. "Darren is a good family friend. He's like a nephew to me, so I have to make sure he's in good hands. Are you still in high school?"

I take Elaine's hand off my leg. "Bridget goes to Cal."

"Oh, really? Why not Stanford? They're not too far from each other."

Elaine knows perfectly well that those are fighting words for some diehard Oskis.

But Bridget doesn't seem ruffled. "I didn't get into Stanford. But even if I did, I still might have chosen Cal."

"Oh, that's silly. Who would choose Cal over Stanford?"

Beneath the table, Elaine rubs her foot along my calf.

"Where did you go to college?" Bridget asks as we're served the first course. "Or did you go to college?"

"I went to Yale. It's even harder to get into than Stanford."

"Is it?" I challenge.

"I'm sure you would have gotten into either."

"I didn't apply to Yale. And like Bridget, I didn't get into Stanford."

"Their loss." She turns to Bridget. "So what are you studying?"

"Public health," Bridget answers.

"How cute. What is that?"

"Elaine's not familiar with a lot of majors," I explain. "She majored in how-to-find-and-marry-rich. That's why she went to an Ivy League school."

Elaine fakes a laugh. "You're so funny, Darren."

Undaunted, Elaine continues to ask questions of Bridget, remarking "cute" every other sentence. I can't wait for dinner to conclude. When Bridget goes to use the restroom before dessert is served, I turn to Elaine.

"Back off Bridget," I tell her.

"My, my, we're testy. Is she not putting out for you?" Elaine puts her hand on my thigh again. "I can— Ow!"

Still holding her wrist tightly, I put her hand on the table. It draws the attention of a few others.

I lean to whisper in Elaine's ear. "Don't sit next to us again."

I get up from the table and wait for Bridget outside the ladies' room.

"What's up?" Bridget asks when she comes out and sees me.

"Don't feel like dessert," I answer.

"Okay. You want to sit by the pool?"

"Sure."

We walk over and settle into a plush sofa before an open fire pit.

"So, how come you didn't throw soda in Elaine's face?" I ask.

"Because I have manners. I don't want to make a scene right before Andrea's wedding and in front of your relatives."

"Fine. But you wanted to, right?"

Bridget grins. "Not really. It was more fun watching you struggle with playing footsies with her."

She knew?

"She won't bother you anymore," I say.

Bridget shrugs. "She doesn't bother me that

much."

"Really?" I don't believe it. After seeing Elaine fawn over me once, Kimberly was ready to tear the woman's hair out. "She was pretty catty to you in a passive-aggressive way."

"That's her issue."

"So how come you didn't have any problems throwing your drink in *my* face?"

She thinks for a moment. "Somehow, you push my buttons more."

I'm okay with that, given I know how to push the right buttons. I pull her into me. Her body next to mine has a calming effect. It feels like everything is right in the world.

Until Bridget asks, "You ever sleep with her?"

I rub my mouth and jaw. Damn women's intuition. "Once," I answer. "Years ago."

"She's still into you."

"You jealous?"

Bridget scrunches up her face. "Why? Just because you slept with her?"

I stare at Bridget. How is she not jealous? The women I've been with have always hated any ex-girlfriends or sex partners of mine. "What if I invited her into a threesome with us?"

"If I wanted a threesome, she would not be my choice."

"Yeah? Who would?"

Bridget cranes her head to look back where we were sitting. She picks out one of the bridesmaids.

"Lisa."

"Why Lisa?"

"She seems fun and doesn't seem to take herself too seriously. Who would you pick?"

This could be dangerous territory to discuss, like answering when a woman asks, "Does this make me look fat?"

"Lisa," I second.

"Why?"

"Her boyfriend's annoying. It would be fun to watch him turn green with envy."

"Is he the world-revolves-around-me-because-I-went-to-Harvard guy?"

"That's the one."

Bridget laughs. I'm surprised we're having a conversation about menage, even if it is hypothetical, without Bridget getting wierded out by it.

"You ever been in a threesome?" I ask, wondering if maybe she's not as wholesome as she appears.

"No. Have you?"

I regret my question now.

She interprets my silence. "You have. Is it something you do a lot of?"

"No."

"You ever do a threesome with Kimberly?"

"Why do you ask?"

"Just curious. Don't worry. I'm not going to judge you."

184

"Does it matter what I did with Kimberly?"

"No."

She leaves it at that. We sit in comfortable silence until a server comes by and asks if we want anything. We both shake our heads.

"How much do I owe you for dinner and room service?" Bridget asks.

"JD took care of dinner. But why are we back on this topic?"

"You said I could help pay for the meals."

"That was before I said we do the trip my way."

"All right. I probably could only afford to pay for two meals anyway."

"One and a half," I correct, recalling she said she has seventy-eight bucks to spare.

"I know I gave you a hard time before coming," she tells me, "but that doesn't mean I don't appreciate all this. It's probably the most amazing trip I'll ever have in my entire life. I'm so grateful, I'll put up with a hundred Elaines."

She rests her head against me, and I kiss the top of her head and smell the shampoo from her earlier shower. Looking out into the horizon, the sparkle of lights in the distant cliffside, I marvel at the view. I've been to Phuket before and looked at similar vistas. But tonight, it looks more special.

My moment of peace and contentment doesn't last long, however. A couple of men are sitting down in the alcove next to ours, and I recognize the voice of Joseph Mok.

185

Mok, sporting a buzz cut and a dark Stefano Ricci blazer, spots me. Preston asks him something, diverting his attention.

Amy and JD plop down on the sofa beside us, both of them holding drinks decorated with a hibiscus flower.

"Hey, we're doing a couples' spa treatment tomorrow," Amy says. "You want to do one, too?"

I look to Bridget, who hesitates, probably because she feels too guilty to indulge in one, so I answer for her. "Sure."

"I thought we could go into town," Bridget says.

"We can do that, too."

"My sister told me I need to go to Jungceylon. I totally want to check it out." She turns to JD. "Can we?"

"'Course, babe," JD answers. He looks over at me. "My aunt try to hit on you again?"

I stare at JD. He had to bring that up?

"OMG, you're not serious?" Amy gasps.

"I think she's had the hots for Darren since he was sixteen."

"That's gross."

"We had Darren over one summer—"

I interrupt. "You want to shut the fuck up?"

Bridget straightens. "What happened?"

JD catches my glare. "Nothing."

"*Something* must have happened."

"I don't want to know," Amy says. "I mean, she's so much *older.*"

"Only by like sixteen years," JD says.

"Still, she's like a cougar."

JD makes cat claws with his hands. "Meow."

"And isn't she related?"

"She married into the Lee family, so she's not a blood relative."

I glance over to where Mok is sitting with Preston and the other groomsmen. Mok is staring at me. He clearly hasn't forgotten what happened between us back in Vietnam. His gaze lowers to Bridget. Instinctively, I tighten my arm around her.

CHAPTER TWENTY-ONE

BRIDGET
Past

"**I** think it's time we gave you a safe word." Still not fully awake, I snuggle into the crook of Darren's arm. The jet lag wasn't so bad, but I was tired after going out clubbing. Andrea had opted for a smaller, more exclusive club, but it still wasn't really my scene. I enjoyed dancing with Darren, but I also had to watch the occasional woman hit on him. Although Elaine wasn't with us, one of the women on the groom's side boldly flirted with Darren as if I wasn't even there.

I was so exhausted by the time we got back around three in the morning that I didn't even bother looking for my pajamas. I just took off my clothes and crawled into bed naked. Darren did the same.

"You have a word you want to use?" he asks.

"No. Do I really need one?" I murmur.

"Yes. Otherwise, I don't know if I've gone too far. And the word has to be unique enough that it won't get lost in the scene."

"Unique? Like…cake?"

"Sure, we can try that."

I move to wrap my arm about his waist and graze his hard-on. "Whoa. You need me to take care of that for you?"

"Hell yes," he replies, his voice gruff with desire.

He pushes my head beneath the covers toward his groin. Fisting the base of his shaft, I start by licking his cock, flicking my tongue over the grooves and flares of the head. Relishing his grunts, I envelop his tip with my mouth and suck, tasting his pre-cum. He pushes my head down to take more of him. I tongue the underside as I go up and down. He groans, grabs me, and positions me over him so that we're in full-fledged 69. Pretty soon, I'm half distracted by what he's doing to me with his tongue and forget my part.

I come off his cock. "Can I come?"

"You're not there yet."

"I know, but I want to ask before you stuff my mouth and claim you can't understand me."

He chuckles, then rolls me under him before returning to the cunnilingus. He pumps his hips, driving his cock deeper. I try my best to relax my throat and hold on to his buttocks. I feel my wetness dripping down to my ass. He seems to

189

notice this, too.

"Good time for the anal plug," he says, then hops out of bed to the bag where he got the Ben Wa balls.

Crap. I had forgotten about that.

He opens a rectangular box and shows me three teardrop-shaped plugs with jeweled hearts at the ends.

"This is a good training set," he explains.

They look fairly harmless, I decide. He takes the smallest one out and lets me hold it in my hand.

I give it back. "That's going to go in my…?"

"Turn around and get on your hands and knees."

After I'm in position, he caresses my back and derriere. "Relax, Bridge."

He rubs the plug along my clit till I'm aroused enough to actually want this. He grabs a buttock and shakes it, then presses the plug into my vagina. He fucks me with the plug a few times before moving it to my back hole.

"Relax," he reminds me, pressing the tip against me. "It's not going to hurt. It's going to feel good."

I can't help it. It just feels weird having anything go *in* a point of *exit*. With his free hand, he fondles my clit before pressing the plug against my sphincter.

"Inhale," he directs. "Now exhale."

On the exhale, he pushes the tip of the plug in.

I stay perfectly still even though I want to squirm away. This feels plain weird.

"Inhale…exhale."

He sinks more of the plug in. Gradually, with each exhale, more and more of the plug is nestled in me until my anus seems to suddenly go from resistance to pulling it in.

"Good girl, Bridge."

I adjust to the fullness faster than I thought I would, until he grasps the end of the plug and wiggles it. Releasing the plug, he gives my buttock a slap. Then he intensifies his fingers against my clit, and the pleasure is *incredible*. I don't know how the plug has anything to do with my clit, but the whole area between my legs is lit. The stimulation at my clit seems to accentuate the butt plug, which responds by echoing the pleasure from my clit. I'm bewildered and ecstatic.

"Can I come? Can I come?" I ask in a hurry.

"Yes."

"Ohhhhhh…"

Fireworks go off between my legs. I don't know what to do with my body. As long as he's touching me, I'm on some other plane of sensation. Eventually, he withdraws his fingers but leaves the plug in.

By the time my climax finally fades, I am more than awake.

*****

191

The rest of the morning, we hang out on the beach and watch the wedding rehearsal. I read through materials for school. We have lunch at the open-air, beachside grill, where I order the turmeric and coriander prawns while Darren opts for the grilled Wagyu. Darren compliments me on not agonizing over the prices. I admit that I feel a little guilty not opting for the least-expensive lunch item, but I think I'm getting used to spending his money.

Darren leans over to me and whispers, "It's going to be more than worth it once we're back at The Lotus."

Halfway through the meal, while I listen to Amy compare this trip to the one her family took to Hong Kong, I see Darren look over to the far side of the restaurant where two men have sat down. I think they might be with the wedding, but Darren doesn't look too happy to see them.

"That's another friend from USC," I overhear JD say to Darren.

Later, I glance over at the two men and see that one of them is looking at Darren with equal displeasure. In fact, they're engaged in a staring contest.

Dessert menu in hand, I draw Darren's attention by saying, "This sticky rice dessert sounds like the one we had at your place."

Lunch ends with no more staring contests, but I

do look over at the other guy twice. Both times, I find him staring at *me.*

"Who was the guy in the restaurant?" I ask Darren as we walk back to our villa.

"No one important," he replies.

"You sure about that? You looked ready to kill him. Either that, or you guys were going to get hot and heavy."

"We don't like each other. There's not much more than that."

I get that guys don't like to get as personal as women, but I feel like there's a whole other side of Darren that I don't know much about. I tell myself that we haven't been together long, a lot of our time is filled with sex, and he's one of those private types. But I'd like to try to peel away some of those layers.

"Just stay away from him," Darren adds.

After lunch is our couples' massage and spa treatment. Even though I've never had so much as a facial, I can't imagine any massage or spa treatment more special than being outside overlooking the sea. First comes a milk bath, then a jasmine rice body scrub, a facial involving jade stones and sacred lotus, and finally an aroma-infused massage with Siamese healing herbs. Any massage would have been a luxury, but each of us has two masseuses working on us. By the time they're done, I feel like relaxed Jell-O.

Back in the women's locker room, wrapped in a

plush spa robe, I retrieve my t-shirt, shorts, and flip-flops from a locker. I hear voices, coming from the other side of a set of lockers, that I recognize: Andrea, another bridesmaid named Moon, and Yu-Jin, the girl who kept hitting on Darren in front of me last night.

"Can you believe the girls Darren and JD brought with them?" Moon asks.

"JD has a different girl like every month," Andrea replies.

"But they must be serious if they brought them here to your wedding."

"Not really. Remember the girl JD brought to my father's 50th in Sydney? He dumped her a week later."

"I mean, that girl Amy is cute, though her clothes could use an upgrade."

"Her clothes are like haute couture compared to what her friend was wearing!" Yu-Jin pipes in. "I saw her wearing a t-shirt and flip-flops that look like they came from Kmart or something."

"What's Kmart?"

"So Darren can't be, like, serious about this girl, right?"

"You keep working it, girl. You could have him dumping her in days, I bet."

"I just hope he's not in some kind of banana phase."

"Darren's not like that," Andrea says. "I think most of the time he's with an Asian woman. And

Bridget's not even white, I think. At least not full white."

Returning from the bathroom, Amy walks up to me at that point. "Hey, what's the matter?"

The other side of the lockers grows quiet.

"I was just thinking about what a beautiful place this is," I answer, "and how lucky JD is to have you because you're not one of those shallow bougie girls with tits for brains. And if JD can't see that, he's not worth it."

Amy smiles. "Ahh, thanks, Bridge. Are you guys going to the rehearsal dinner tonight?"

"I don't think so. I told Linda I'd work on a grant application."

"You're so dedicated. They should give you a pay raise."

After I meet up with Darren to head back to our villa, I bring up the grant application I want to work on.

"But I don't want you to miss out on the rehearsal dinner because of me," I add.

"Something the matter?" Darren asks.

"Well, everyone here knows everyone else. It might be nice for the rehearsal dinner to be more intimate without a stranger like me."

"There'll be over forty people at the rehearsal dinner. How intimate can it get?"

"I also told Coretta I'd give her a call. I only texted her yesterday."

Darren didn't push it.

Once we were back in our villa, Darren gets ready for the rehearsal dinner. While he takes a shower, I decide to soak in the bathtub, which is right next to the window with the view of the beach.

"Does JD have a lot of ex-girlfriends?" I ask as nonchalantly as I can.

"What do you consider 'a lot?'"

Unable to settle on a good metric, I ask instead, "Does he kind of move from one girl to the next?"

"Why are you asking?"

"He's dating my friend. I'm curious to know more about him. So, does he?"

"Sometimes."

"Has he ever had a long-term relationship?"

Darren sighs. "Maybe he hasn't met the right person."

"Does he *want* to meet the right person?"

"I don't know. It's not the kind of thing guys talk about a lot."

I get the sense that Darren's a tad uncomfortable, which doesn't inspire me with confidence where JD is concerned.

"Amy's having a lot of fun with him," I say, and study his reaction.

"Yeah. I bet their sex is good. Not as good as ours, though."

"I bet he doesn't make her call him 'sir.'"

Darren steps out of the shower and wraps a towel around his waist. "You'll have to ask Amy about that."

"What's with the 'sir' thing anyway?" I ask, eying the way the water glistens on his bronzed skin. My gaze rakes over his pecs and six-pack.

"It reinforces the Dom-sub relationship."

"Will I ever get to be the Dom?"

"If I allow it."

"Since we've already ventured into BDSM, do I still have to give you a night at your club?"

"You better believe it."

I sink into the water. So far, I've been able to handle everything he's thrown at me. I wonder how Yu-Jin would react to Darren's penchant for kink. I envision her fighting with Elaine over Darren. Who would win?

A surprising stab of jealousy shoots through me, but I quell it. Like I told Amy, if he can't appreciate what he's got, it's his loss.

Darren takes off his towel and steps into the bathtub.

"Don't you need to get ready for the rehearsal dinner?" I inquire.

"I'll get there. After we fuck."

"It sounds so romantic when you say it like that."

He sits down with a smirk. Reaching for me, he pulls me between his spread legs and has me lie against his chest. With one hand, he fondles my breast. With the other, he strokes me between my thighs. I sigh at how good it feels to be wrapped in

197

the steamy water, his muscular arms around me, my clit caressed to perfection, his erection pressed against my backside.

After he brings me to full arousal, he has me get on my hands and knees. The bathtub is deep, with the water level teasing the edge. I have to crane my neck to keep my head above water. He kneels behind me, and I feel his cock at my entry. He buries himself in me gradually, then circles his thumb around my other hole, reminding me that earlier I lost that virginity.

"I can't wait to be inside there," he murmurs, slowly bucking his hips.

I can. The butt plug was a good size, and still much smaller than him.

"Touch yourself," he commands.

Not wanting to lose the momentum for my arousal, I happily reach for my clit. His thrusting causes the water to splash into my face. It's distracting, making me lose track of my place.

"You want some breath play?" he asks.

Remembering how intensely I came the time he covered my mouth and nose to keep me quiet so that my other housemate, Simone, didn't hear anything, I say okay.

Darren fists his hand in my hair. "Take a good breath. Now hold it."

I thought he was just going to do what he did before. Instead, he dunks my head under water while he shoves himself into me.

When he pulls my head back up, I gasp loudly, mostly because I panicked. He waits for me to collect myself.

"Good breath. And hold."

Wait! We're doing this again? I quickly take a breath before he plunges me back in.

"That's enough," I sputter when he pulls me out.

"You have to use your safety word."

Safety word. What was my safety word?

"Take a breath and hold."

I remember the safety word when I'm underwater. As soon as I'm back out, I say, "Cake!"

Water streams down my face. He releases my hair and wipes my face. I make a mental note not to forget my safety word next time.

He pulls me up so I'm on my knees. I'm glad my face is no longer near the water. He gropes my breasts, then turns my face around to take my mouth. Still recovering from the breath play, it takes me several minutes before I engage in the long, wet kiss. Fitting a hand between my thighs, he rubs my clit.

"Can I come?" I whisper while his mouth continues to devour me.

"Yes, Bridge."

He pinches a nipple harshly. My climax follows seconds after. I quake against him, his hands on my mound and on a breast, my pussy spasming over his cock, which is still buried inside me. When

199

I'm done, my body still throbs in multiple places.

Darren withdraws his cock and sits back down. "Suck me off."

I settle on my hands and knees between his legs, but his lower body is completely beneath water, which means more breath play. I take a deep breath, hold it, and go down on him. This might take a while, since I have to come up for air every now and then, so I use my hands and jerk him off when I need a breath. From his grunts, I gather he's getting closer and closer to his climax. He also starts holding my head in place when my mouth is wrapped around his shaft.

Feeling as if I'm unable to hold my breath much longer, I start to struggle. Of course, I can't utter my safety word, and that's a little scary. But when I start slapping his arm, he lets me up. He raises his hips so that his cock is closer to the surface. I intensify my sucking, work his shaft with one hand and grab his balls with the other. He drops an oath and starts bucking in short, rapid motions, sending water into my face again. I taste his cum and let it drip out of my mouth, surprised he hasn't ordered me to swallow it. I suspect that day will come.

With a sigh, he sinks back into the water. I settle against him and we sit in the tub for a while, even though the water has grown tepid.

The ringing of his cell prompts us to get out. It stops as he wraps a towel around him. Walking over to the bathroom counter, he picks up his phone to see who called.

Seeing the expression on his face, I ask, "What's the matter?"

He turns to me. "My mom's here."

CHAPTER TWENTY-TWO

BRIDGET
Past

I put on the summer dress Cheryl bought to meet Mrs. Sharon Lee. I feel a little nervous, more so when I see her for the first time standing with one of the other wedding guests. Sharon is tall, beautiful and has a quiet glamor to her.

"Mother," Darren greets her.

Her eyes light up upon seeing him, though there are no hugs or kisses. Amy explained to me once that many Asian families are not big on public displays of affection.

She narrows her eyes at her son. "You look dark. How are you so tan when it's winter?"

"I was in Hawaii not that long ago."

"You got too much sun then."

"Mother, this is Bridget Moore."

She looks me over, and I get the feeling I'm not what she expected, but her tone is friendly enough when she says, "Nice to meet you."

The other guest, Mr. Liao, is a friend of the bride's family. He hasn't seen Darren in a while and asks how things are going. He politely asks a few questions of me, and says, "Go, Bears" when I tell him I go to Cal.

When I tell him I'm studying public health, he asks if I plan to go to medical school. I explain I'm more interested in the policy side of health, and he responds by asking, "Don't you get paid more as a doctor?"

"You do, and you're also less likely to receive death threats than a public health officer," I reply.

"So why would you want to be in public health?"

"I think the last pandemic showed that we need public health expertise."

He either agrees with my answer or decides it's not worth talking about anymore, because he turns to Sharon. "You must be proud of Darren. Word is he might follow in his old man's footsteps."

I feel Darren stiffen beside me. Is it my imagination or did a chill just fall over us?

Sharon turns to me. "So, tell me more about public health. Besides pandemics, what else does it involve?"

"A lot. Everything from food to hospital care to environmental health to racial inequities. I could go on and on."

"You sound passionate about it. You must be a good student."

She raises a brow at Darren.

"'Unlike my son' is what that look means," Darren says to me.

"Grades aren't as important anymore," says Mr. Liao. "As we can see from Darren's success."

Sharon doesn't seem to want to talk about her son. She looks past us and says with a grim curl of her lips, "I see that Elaine is here."

"Of course," Darren replies. "She's the bride's aunt."

Elaine spots Darren's mother. "Is that Sharon Lee?"

She comes over and drips with obsequiousness. "I thought you couldn't make it."

Sharon looks to Darren. "Something came up, and I had to be here."

Elaine turns to Darren, too. "You aren't at the rehearsal dinner."

"Why aren't *you* at the rehearsal dinner?"

"I thought I left my clutch out here. I guess I should go look for it."

Yes, you should, was the look Sharon gave her. After Elaine leaves, Sharon says, "I should go check into my room. I have one of the cliffside villas. It was nice to meet you, Bridget."

"It's nice that your mom could make the wedding," I comment.

"Yeah."

I can tell something else is on his mind, but I don't want to pry. At least not all the time.

The following day, we get to do the touristy stuff like visiting the Big Buddha, a giant statue atop Mount Nagakerd; Wat Chalong, a colorful Buddhist temple; and Jungceylon, the shopping mall that Amy wanted to go to. Although the mall is impressive, with a fountain that one might find in Vegas, I prefer the street markets in Malin Plaza or Bangla Road.

When we get back to the resort in the late afternoon, JD convinces Darren to go golfing with the groom and a few others. I decide to take my laptop to a lounge chair by the infinity pool to work on a grant application. It's not easy getting into work when there's such a majestic view in front of me, but I eventually turn on my computer. Being old, it has a battery life of only one hour before it needs recharging, so I need to crank.

"Hey."

Looking up, I see it's the guy from the restaurant.

"Hi," I say cautiously.

He sits down on the lounge chair next to me and extends a hand. "Joseph Mok."

I shake it. "Bridget."

"So you Darren's girlfriend?"

I don't think I'm in official girlfriend territory, but for some reason I don't want to say otherwise to Joseph.

"We like each other," I reply. I'm curious to know what happened between the two of them.

"How do you know Darren?"

"Mutual acquaintances."

"Like the groom?"

"Something like that."

A server comes by. Joseph orders a drink and sits back.

"Do you guys go back a ways?" I ask.

"Yeah. We met in Vietnam. You can probably tell Darren doesn't like me much."

"I noticed you guys looking at each other the other day."

"I got angry with him because he slept with my girlfriend."

Oh. That would explain the lack of love lost. I'm surprised Joseph just came right out and said it.

"Darren serious about you?" Joseph asks as he appraises me.

"I can't answer for him."

He looks disgruntled. "Where'd Darren find you?"

"Find me? You mean, like on the discount rack at a secondhand store?" Not wanting more pointed questions from him, I turn to my computer. "I should get back to my work."

"I asked a simple question. No need to get bitchy about it."

Deciding I'd rather work back at the villa, I close my computer. But then I spot Sharon coming my way. "Hi, Mrs. Lee."

She sits down on the lounge chair on my other

side. Next to her stunning gold sheer caftan worn over a stylish plunge-neck one-piece, I feel frumpy in my t-shirt and gym shorts. Joseph gets up and leaves without a word.

"Where's Darren?" Sharon asks.

"Golfing."

"He's not much of a golfer. Swimming is his sport."

That explains his broad shoulders.

"Really? I didn't know that."

"I'm sure there's a lot of things you don't know about my son."

I'm not sure how to take that.

She eyes my laptop. "What are you working on?"

"A grant application for my internship. We're trying to get funding to purchase refrigerated vans."

"What for?"

"Our food recovery program. There's a ton of food that goes to waste each day that low-income families could use. Our goal is to collect the food from places like restaurants and retailers, and transport it to distribution programs."

"That stuff doesn't exist already? Don't soup kitchens do that?"

"Surprisingly, we'd be the first to do this at a county level. The local food banks aren't able to house fresh fruits and vegetables. They distribute canned and packaged foods, but people can't subsist on that kind of food, which tends to be nutrient deficient and contains additives and other ingredients that are detrimental to health. Because something as simple as not getting fresh produce leads to chronic illnesses, low-income families end up needing more medical care. That's why another program we have is called a food pharmacy."

Sharon stares at me. "How did you and my son meet?"

"My friend, Amy, is dating JD."

"Right. JD likes them young and cute, like your friend."

Wondering if Sharon might be more informative than Darren, I ask, "Has he had a lot of girlfriends that are young and cute?"

Sharon looks out at the view. "I shouldn't have said anything. It's really none of my business who he dates."

"Actually, I'm curious. I'd like to know my friend's dating a good guy."

"What is a 'good guy?'"

"Someone who will care about her and treat her right."

"Do you feel like Darren is a 'good guy?'"

Is that a strange question for a mother to ask? For some reason, I want to ask the same of her.

"I haven't seen any indications to suggest that he *isn't* a good guy."

"Couldn't you say that about most men you meet?"

"You've got a point. I guess it's just an instinct I have."

She brings her knees up. "What if you're wrong?"

I shrug. "Then I'm wrong. We move on."

"Are you in love with him?"

It's a pointed question not unlike the ones Joseph was asking, but as the mother, she has a right to ask it.

"Honestly, we haven't known each other that long," I reply. "I'm not sure why he chose to invite me, but I'm appreciative that he did."

"What do you mean, you're not sure why he invited you?"

"I just picture him with a woman more like his ex-girlfriend, Kimberly. Someone a little more glamorous. I think I'm a little nerdy for his usual tastes."

By her brief silence, I think she agrees with my assessment. "You don't think you're good enough for my son?"

"Not at all! I know I'm not the prettiest or wealthiest person he could be dating, but I bring a lot to the table. Not to be immodest, but maybe I'm a breath of fresh air for Darren. Someone different."

She seems to weigh what I say. "Don't take this the wrong way, but you *are* different."

Kind of hard not to take a statement like that the wrong way, but I don't detect any antagonism in her tone.

"Darren and I haven't known each other long enough to be too serious," I assure her. "And if we *were* to become more serious, you don't have to worry about me. I care deeply about the people in my life, my family and friends, and I'd always have their interests at heart."

I must have spoken with more earnestness than I'd intended because she doesn't respond right away.

"Tell me about your family," she finally says.

I tell her about how my grandmother raised me because my father had passed away when I was just a baby.

"She lives in Europe with her boyfriend," I answer, when she asks about my mother.

By the end of our conversation, I can't tell if Mrs. Lee approves of me or not.

CHAPTER TWENTY-THREE

DARREN
Past

"Where's Bridget?" my mother asks when I join her on the balcony of her villa.

"In one of the cooking classes learning how to make pad thai and curry," I reply. I sit down next to her to watch the sunset.

"I had a chat with her this afternoon."

She waits for my reaction, but I don't provide her one.

"She seems nice."

Knowing that's not all she has to say, I wait for her to continue.

She cuts to the chase. "Too nice."

I don't say anything, though I happen to agree with her.

"Really. What are you doing with someone like her?" my mother asks.

"You'd prefer I was with Kimberly?"

"No! Well...Kimberly would at least be okay with your triad association."

"I thought you didn't want me with the triad anymore?"

"I don't. Tommy tried to talk me into being okay about you taking your father's place in counterfeiting. He made it sound like you were going to do it."

"Is that why you're here? You want to talk me out of it?"

"Yes! You know you could get up to twenty years?"

"That's not so bad."

She makes a face. "I did not spend eighteen years raising you, then sending you off to college so that you can end up in jail. What would happen to Bridget if you went to jail?"

"She'd end up like you, is my guess. A rich widow."

"With a broken heart. Is that what you want for your girlfriend?"

"She's not my...we might not even be together in a month."

"Why are you together now? I thought you were coming stag."

"I thought it'd be fun to invite Bridget."

"You should be careful. What if she falls in love with you?"

"She's too levelheaded to do that."

"Women are capable of a lot of irrational

behavior."

"Speaking from experience?"

"I thought *I* was levelheaded."

I stretch my legs out. "You're different. You were okay with Dad being in the triad until he went to jail. Bridget doesn't even drink. Hell, I had to bend over backwards just to get her to accept an all-expenses-paid trip to Thailand. What woman in her right mind doesn't automatically say 'yes' to an invitation like that?"

"You should call it off with her sooner rather than later. Before you get too serious about each other."

"You worried about me?"

"It's for her benefit, too. She's one of those do-gooders. You'll mess up her life."

For some reason, that thought doesn't sit well with me. Maybe my mom's right about calling it off sooner rather than later.

"So what did you tell Lee Hao Young?" my mother asks next.

"I told him I'd think about it."

"You don't have to follow in your father's footsteps."

"I don't want to run The Lotus for the rest of my life."

"So do something else. You have a degree from UCLA."

"To do what? Work for some boring-ass company? Risk golden handcuffs instead of jail?"

"If you don't like boring, why are you with Bridget?"

I surprise myself when I look at her and say, "She's not boring."

My mother grows silent before saying, "I know you won't necessarily take my advice. You know what will make me happy when it comes to the *Jing San*. And if you do stick around with the triad, you're better off letting Bridget go."

*****

Per Bridget's request, we hit the street markets for dinner. JD and Amy opted to dine at one of the five-star restaurants and go clubbing afterward, and I'm glad to have Bridget to myself. She gawks at the long line of food vendors stretching through the Laird Yai and insists on treating me to moo ping and som tam from a street vendor.

"It's the one meal I can afford to do so," she insists.

For dessert, she passes on the coconut ice cream served in a hot dog bun in favor of a roti stuffed with bananas and sweetened with condensed milk.

"So what'd you do while I was in class?" Bridget asks as we stroll beneath strings of lights stretching across the street.

"Talked with my mom," I replied.

"That's nice. What did you guys talk about?"

"You."

"Really? What did she say about me?"

"That I'm not good enough for you."

Bridget does a double-take, then chuckles. She thinks I'm joking.

"I had a chat with your mom today, too," she tells me.

"My mentioned that. When did that happen?"

"While you were golfing. We sat by the pool together."

"What did you guys talk about?"

"You."

I smirk. "What'd she say?"

She thinks for a moment. "She asked if I was in love with you."

I hesitate, because I'm not sure I want to know the answer, but Bridget doesn't seem the type of person to fall for someone too easily, unlike her friend Amy.

"What did you say?" I ask.

"I said 'hell, no, I'm just using him to get a free trip to Thailand.'"

I laugh.

"In reality, I told her we haven't known each other long," she reveals.

"So the answer was 'no.'"

She pauses, then asks, "Did you want a different answer?"

I also pause. I've never regarded crowded street markets, made muggy by the mass of people, filled with a variety of smells both aromatic and pungent, as romantic. But looking at Bridget, that was the way I felt. Like I did want a different answer.

I brush it off. "'Course not."

Like me, she seems faintly disappointed, then tries to lighten the tension by joking, "I told her we were just about the sex."

"Good."

We continue walking, but when her hand grazes mine, I decide to take it.

CHAPTER TWENTY-FOUR

DARREN
Past

I had just come as close to making love as sex gets for me, and Bridget ruins the moment by telling me afterward that she talked to Joseph Mok.

"I told you to stay away from the guy," I say as we lie in bed.

Outside the bedroom window, the moon is nearly full, a bright white coin in a cloudless sky.

"Why?" Bridget asks.

"Because I said so."

She groans. "Just because I let you do your BDSM thing doesn't mean you get to boss me around outside of sex."

"My BDSM thing?" *She has no idea what "my BDSM thing" really entails.*

"Besides, it's not like I went up to him," she continues. "He came and sat down next to me at the pool."

"Could you have walked away?"

"Yes, but that would have been rude at first."

I roll my eyes.

"Okay, I was a little curious about him since you seemed to dislike him so much," she admits. "Did you really sleep with his girlfriend?"

That fucking douche told her that?

"I didn't know she was with him at first," I reply.

"'At first?'"

"He was being a jerk, getting up in my face even after I apologized. We got into a fight, and yeah, I slept with her the next day. Didn't plan to, but she invited me up to her place."

I could have kept things simple by lying, but for some reason I didn't feel like lying to Bridget. Maybe because she'd sniff out the truth. I don't know.

"No wonder he doesn't like you!"

I look at her in disbelief. "You're taking *his* side?"

"If you think about it...wait, what kind of fight did you get in?"

"I broke his nose."

Her eyes widen. "Well, that just adds to it!"

"The guy's a grade-A asshole."

"I don't disagree, but breaking his nose?"

I growl and look away. "It's a guy thing."

"Did you try diplomacy first?"

"No, I did not try any fucking diplomacy. We

were in a dive bar, not the United Nations. I was drunk, he was drunk. If it makes you happy, I learned my lesson. I don't get drunk like that anymore. At least not in public bars in foreign countries."

Bridget is quiet, and I regret my tone of voice, but I'm still upset that Joseph spoke with her. Grabbing the panties I took off her earlier, I flip her onto her stomach and tie her wrists behind her with the underwear.

"What else did he say to you?" I ask.

"That was pretty much it."

I lie on top of her, tug at her earlobe with my teeth, and slip my had between her thighs. "I think there was more."

"He said he knew you didn't like him. Oh! That feels good…"

"What else?"

"Um, he asked if you were serious about me, and…said I was bitchy."

I stop fondling her clit. "What?!"

"I didn't like his questions and told him I wanted to get back to my work."

I wish I could have been there to witness exactly how their exchange went. I don't like that Mok called Bridget bitchy, but I'm glad she was antagonistic toward him.

"That it?" I press, caressing her clit again.

"Yes, I swear."

Satisfied she's telling the truth, I pull her down

219

past the edge of the bed so that her feet touch the floor and her ass rounds the end of the bed nicely.

"Don't move," I tell her.

I didn't bring any toys for impact play, so I look around to see what there is. I go into the bathroom and return with her hairbrush, which is made of bamboo and has a rectangular head, practically a paddle.

"How many?"

"How many *what*?" she asks.

"Spanks. For disobeying me when I told you to stay away from Joseph Mok."

"You're kidding, right?"

"You want me to pick the number?"

She eyes the brush I hold. "You spanking me with that?"

I slap the flat side of the brush into my other hand. "If you pick a number that's too low, I'll add twenty to it."

Her eyes widen. "What's considered too low?"

"Below what you can handle."

"I've never been spanked by a hairbrush before!"

I sit down next to her and caress the curve of her ass. "Do your best guess."

"Can I see what one feels like first?"

A fair enough request. I rub her ass cheeks, warming her up, then reach below for her clit and folds. I caress her till she's good and wet.

"That feels reeeeally good," she croons.

With my hand, I smack her lightly on the buttocks. Her ass is perfection. I don't like them too hard or muscular, and I don't like them flabby. Hers is incredibly smooth, too. Not a single pimple or blemish. I lean over and kiss the cheeks. I lick, mouth and grope the orbs. She should be warmed up now.

"Here's your sample," I tell her before smacking the brush against a buttock.

She yelps.

"How was that?" I inquire.

"Not too bad."

"So how many can you take?"

"Twelve maybe?"

It's more than I thought she would say. "Twelve, it is."

I caress the other buttock before spanking it with the brush. I land a second blow to the previous buttock.

She gasps. "That one hurt more."

I massage the spheres and explain, "It'll hurt more as your ass becomes more and more sensitive."

"I didn't know that!"

"Now you know."

I spank each half twice. A beautiful pink coloring starts to surface.

"How did that feel?" I ask.

"They really sting."

"You're halfway there already."

I tap the brush gently on one cheek. She tenses, but I move to lightly slapping the other cheek. When she relaxes, I give her rump a good wallop. She cries out and shuffles her feet. After letting the sting settle in, I spank the other side. Her hands instinctively move to cover her rear, but I pin her wrists in place as I deliver two more smacks with greater force. She yelps and squirms. Her legs bend beneath her.

"Straighten your legs," I tell her.

With a groan, she returns to her previous position and lifts her ass higher when I tell her to. I turn the brush over and tap the bristles to her rump. She makes a face.

"I'm throwing that hairbrush away," she grumbles.

"You don't think I can find something else to spank you with?" I ask. I turn the brush back around. "Last two. And when we're done, you say, 'Thank you, sir.'"

"To pour salt in the wound. That the sadistic icing on the cake?"

"As a show of appreciation that I've taken the time to teach you better."

She rolls her eyes.

"That kind of attitude just earned you two extra spanks," I tell her.

Her body jumps when I deliver the final four whacks.

"Shit!" she swears through clenched teeth,

burying her face in the bed.

Some Doms don't let their subs swear, but I don't have a problem with it. I assess the redness on her backside. There's no bruising, but it was only fourteen smacks. Some women do bruise easily, but Bridget seems to have tolerated the spanking well. Her ass may burn for a bit, but it won't be painful enough that she can't sit.

"What do you say?" I ask her.

She turns her head and gives me a small glare. "Thank you, sir."

"What's the lesson?"

"To stay away from Joseph Mok."

Setting aside the brush, I fondle her between the legs. "Did you like the spanking?"

"Not particularly."

"You did well, though. So now you get rewarded."

I alternate between sinking two digits into her and rubbing her clit.

"I like what you're doing now."

"If I make you feel good, would you take a spanking again in the future?"

She thinks about it. "Would you use a hairbrush again?"

"Maybe. I prefer impact toys like paddles, crops and canes to everyday household items. The cane leaves really nice purple streaks."

I grope a buttock with my free hand, imagining her ass decorated in black and blue.

"It would also depend on the number of spanks," she says.

"Don't worry. We'd work our way up to higher numbers."

"Higher numbers? Like what?"

"I haven't counted once I pass a hundred."

"A hundred?! Are you serious?"

I intensify the masturbating. "I think you could make it there."

She doesn't answer. Probably fixated on her impending climax. Except she hasn't asked to come yet. Which would mean another punishment, but I don't want to overdo it in one session. I slow my hand. A minute later, she requests permission to come.

"Yes," I answer, "on my command."

I step away from her and go over to my bag to retrieve a vibrator. My cock is definitely up for another go. Standing behind her, I rub my tip along her pussy. She feels so good all wet and slippery against me. I tease her clit with my cock before sinking in. She moans as I rock my hips in long, drawn thrusts.

I turn on the vibrator. "When you come, I want you to come hard, got that?"

"Yes. I mean, yes, sir."

I slap my groin into her still blushing ass before nestling the vibrator against her.

She writhes beneath me. "Oh-my-God-I'm-going-to-come."

I retract the vibrator slightly. "Hold it."

She strains and pants. "I..."

"Hold it."

She goes silent.

I press the vibrator deeper into her. "Now."

Her body actually started spasming before I gave her the go-ahead, but it was close enough. She screams into the bed while I slam my way home, the sound of smacking flesh drowned only by the sound of the bed hitting the wall. It feels like sunshine bursting through my body as I pump furiously. Draining myself into her is my highest craving in that moment.

But even though it feels so damn good to empty myself deep within her, I know this same craving will be back. Over and over again, I'm going to have to fulfill this need for her. And except for the times I wished my father were still alive, I can't remember wanting anything more.

CHAPTER TWENTY-FIVE

BRIDGET
Past

"**I**t's okay, you can say it," I tell Cheryl, who has stopped by the villa to help me dress while Darren, already dressed in his Stefano Ricci tux with satin peak lapels, sits on an armchair outside.

Earlier, Cheryl had booked an appointment in the beauty salon to have my hair and makeup done, and maybe she thought I wouldn't know how to put on the strapless peplum gown with a sweetheart neckline.

"Darren's like a ten out of ten, and I'm lucky to hit a seven," I say. Given what a big deal Darren made of my ugly sweater the first time we met, he hasn't actually denigrated my clothing choices since then.

That a guy who is as well-groomed and attired as Darren is hanging out with someone like me shows he looks beyond the superficial. But will it last?

"You look beautiful," Cheryl says as she zips up my gown.

"Thank you. It's all due to you. You have great taste in clothes. This dress is amazing."

She smiles and picks up a gauze-like scarf, which she wraps around my upper arms—making it look like the gown comes with off-shoulder sleeves—and ties at my back.

"You're the one wearing it," she says.

"Do you have to dress up all his girlfriends?" I joke.

She shakes her head. Probably because they don't need help in this department like I do. It's not that I don't like nice fashion, but I do like my comfort when it comes to clothing. BDSM is another story. I'm surprised I can tolerate it so far, but the more hardcore stuff might be another story.

Cheryl removes a velvet box from a paper bag, saying, "Darren said you wouldn't accept jewelry, so I'll let you borrow mine."

She opens the box and shows me a necklace of black and white diamonds with dangling earrings to match.

My mouth drops. "I can't wear those! I couldn't take it if something were to happen to them"

"You have to," she replies. "Darren said my year-end bonus depends on you looking your best."

"This is too much," I murmur, but I take the jewels and put them on.

"Now you're ready," Cheryl pronounces.

I look at her with gratitude. "Thank you. I'm sure you went above and beyond your job description as club manager."

"I do a lot of things for Darren besides managing his club. Now, go show Darren."

Letting out a breath, I walk out onto the veranda where Darren is sitting. He looks up and doesn't say anything at first. I worry that maybe one of the earrings fell off or that the lady in the beauty salon overdid the makeup.

Darren rises slowly, still silent.

"Is my lipstick smudged?" I wonder, and open my clutch to find a mirror.

He puts his hand over mine and leans in to say in my ear. "You look stunning."

I blush. Okay, I get the desire to dress up all the time, especially if one can get this kind of reaction.

"You, too," I return. "Did you really make Cheryl's bonus contingent on me wearing her jewelry?"

"No, I didn't" he says. He looks to Cheryl, who has been standing to the side. "Clever."

I gawk over at Cheryl. She tricked me?

"We better get going. We don't want to be late."

When we arrive where other wedding guests have congregated, waiting to be seated, I can't help but take some satisfaction in the surprised looks on the faces of Yu-Jin and Moon.

"You make a lovely couple," says Mr. Liao as he greets me and Darren.

Amy hurries over and tugs me away. "OMG, Bridget! You look gorgeous! You are so lucky that you got a new wardrobe with this trip. Darren must be seriously into you."

"I wish he hadn't, to be honest."

"Why?!"

"It makes me feel, I don't know, like his plaything, this doll that he dresses up so he doesn't have to be embarrassed by me."

"I wouldn't mind if JD dressed me up."

"He doesn't have to. You always look amazing."

"You think so? I actually wish I had brought a different dress, something a little sexier, like what she's wearing."

I look over at a pretty young woman who looks eighteen, smiling and laughing with some other wedding guests.

"She was totally flirting with JD last night at the club," Amy tells me. "I went to the ladies' room and when I came back, she and JD were laughing together."

I can tell Amy is concerned. I want to assure her it was probably nothing, but what if it wasn't?

"Do you know anything about her?" I ask.

"Just that she goes to Cornell," Amy says.

"Then she'll be out of sight soon enough."

"I guess. Are you sure you don't want to stay longer than a week?"

I would love to see more of Phuket. Earlier in the day, Darren and I went canoeing and snorkeling. But I don't want to overstay my welcome. Nor do I want to witness more of Elaine or Yu-Jin hitting on Darren.

"I'd like to," I reply, "but I already feel guilty taking a week off."

"Oh, they're seating the guests now. I've got to be up front with JD."

Amy leaves me. I look for Darren and see that Yu-Jin is talking to him. He manages to disengage himself from her, only to wind up being accosted by Elaine a few steps later. I'm not thrilled to see it, but I manage to shake my head and laugh. The trials and tribulations of being attractive.

"What's so amusing?" asks Sharon as she stands beside me.

"Your son," I answer. "He can't make it ten feet without a woman accosting him."

Sharon follows my line of sight and frowns. "And you're okay with this?"

"I don't think it's my choice. I just gotta trust he'll do the right thing."

"And you trust him?"

I think for a moment. "So far, yes. And if I turn out to be wrong, then I'd rather know sooner than later."

"That's very practical."

"If I was going to get jealous over every woman who flirts with your son, I think I'd be exhausted."

We watch Elaine put a hand on Darren's arm.

"If she weren't JD's aunt…" Sharon murmurs.

"Do you want to rescue him or should I?" I ask.

"You do it. I'll come in as backup if needed."

I walk over to Darren and loop my arm around his. Elaine doesn't look pleased to see me.

"Come on, bae," I say to Darren, "they're seating the guests now, and your mom is waiting for us."

He raises his brow at my use of "bae." I pull him away from Elaine and over to Sharon, who gives me a quick smile. We find seats in the third row.

The ceremony, held under a canopy of shimmering gauze accented with bouquets of orchids and Siamese tulips, is breathtakingly beautiful. The bride looks stunning in a hip-hugging gown with a mermaid flare. At the end, over a dozen doves are released. I've only been to one wedding that I can remember, the marriage of Aunt Coretta's eldest. It took place at a local Baptist church in Oakland, and the reception was held in a town hall. Although it wasn't as fancy as the present wedding, it had heart and joy.

A separate reception area lit by torches and open fire pits has been set up on the beach as well. A five-course dinner is followed by dancing and live music. I sit at a table with Mr. Liao, Cheryl, JD, Amy, Sharon, Darren, and, thankfully, no Elaine or Yu-Jin. I get the chance to chat a little more with Sharon, whose polite aloofness seems to have warmed a little toward me.

A live band plays after dinner and takes a break when the wedding cake, a jaw-dropping spectacle of Swarovski crystals and gold dusting, is brought out. Per Chinese tradition, the bride is on her third outfit for the reception, a sexy golden qipao with slits on both sides.

"If I marry JD, I would want a wedding like this," Amy whispers to me.

JD is busy texting on his phone at the moment. Sharon is on the dance floor with Mr. Liao. As is Cheryl. When JD is done, he grabs Amy to dance. I'm still finishing my slice of wedding cake when Elaine comes over, a drink in hand, and sits down next to me, where Amy sat. She leans over as if I'm not even there to talk to Darren.

"I heard your mother is leaving tomorrow," Elaine says. "She was barely here."

"She's helping to take care of a relative in Singapore," Darren replies.

"But to fly all the way here and only stay for two days?"

"It's only two hours to Singapore."

"Still. You know one of my nieces is getting married in wine country this September. You have any recommendations?"

"On what?"

"Anything. You're not that far from places like Napa and Healdsburg, right?"

Tired of having Elaine's perfume underneath my nose, I interject, "You want to switch seats?"

Elaine looks surprised to see that I exist. "Oh, sure."

Darren frowns at me. "Finish that cake soon."

I flash him a "good luck" smile and take my plate of cake. As she gets up and tries to scoot in front of me, part of her drink spills onto my dress.

"I thought you were going behind me," she explains.

I can't tell if it was an accident or not. Either way, I'm done with Elaine's company and am glad to have an excuse to leave.

"I'll go back to the villa and change," I tell Darren.

"I'll go with—" Darren starts, but is interrupted by Elaine waving over a young woman.

"Stella! Come over here! You should talk to Darren about your wedding."

"I won't be long," I assure Darren.

I head back to the villa and think through which of my outfits is nice enough for the wedding reception. I guess the sundress will have to do. Just before I open the sliding door, I hear a sound behind me. So Darren managed to extricate himself from Elaine.

But it's not Darren. It's Joseph Mok.

His tuxedo is an ocean-blue jacket with black pants. He stands so close to me that I can detect the faint smell of alcohol on him.

"Can I help you?" I ask in a tone that indicates I'm not ecstatic to see him.

"You weren't very nice to me the other day," he drawls.

"You were asking a lot of personal questions."

"Didn't mean you have to be nasty."

I hate that the word "nasty" has become en vogue with men who don't like it when women assert themselves. Of course, the men get away with being obnoxious bullies with much less reproach.

"I'm sorry you felt that way," I say. "I think we're just not simpatico."

He reaches for me. "You can make it up to me."

I push him away. Alarm shoots up my spine.

He grabs me again, growling, "What does Darren see in you?"

Recalling a move from a self-defense class, I jab the heel of my palm into his chin.

His head recoils, and he lets go. I take the opportunity to run away, back to the reception area.

Seeing me, Darren strides over. "Bridget, what's wrong?"

I catch my breath first before answering. "I had a run-in with Joseph Mok."

His features darken and his jaw tenses. "What happened?"

His expression makes me nervous, so I try to downplay the incident till Darren's settled down. "Just being a jerk."

Darren doesn't buy it or doesn't care. "Where is

234

he?"

We both scan the reception but don't see him. Seeing a woman approach from outside the area, Darren walks up to her. "You seen Joseph Mok?"

"I saw him go into the men's room," she answers. "The one behind the restaurant."

Darren starts in that direction. I scurry to keep up.

"What are you going to do?" I ask.

Darren doesn't answer.

I grab his arm, but he keeps going.

"I'm okay," I say. "Nothing really happened."

I have a pit in my stomach. Of course, I want to see Joseph get a reckoning, but I don't want Darren to end up in jail.

We reach the restrooms. I grab Darren again. "You didn't let me finish—"

Joseph steps out of the men's room.

Darren slams him up against the wall. "Don't come near her ever again."

"Chill, man," Joseph replies. "Trust me, I won't."

I try to wrestle his hold off Joseph. "Darren! Leave it! It's not worth it."

Darren's lips are pressed into a grim line, but he releases Joseph and allows me to pull him away.

Joseph straightens his bowtie and mutters, "Who'd want your nasty ho anyway?"

Turning around, Darren lands a right hook to the side of Joseph's head.

A trio of women who have just emerged from

the ladies' room scream.

"Go get help!" I tell one of them as Joseph rushes Darren.

The men fall to the sand. Joseph returns the punch. Running over, I yank on his collar to try to pull him off. It doesn't work, so I take off one of my shoes and start hitting him over the head with it. Darren rolls away and gets back onto his feet. At first, Joseph tries to protect his head, but when I pause, he elbows me across the mouth. I stumble back. My whole head rings. I taste blood.

A woman screams again.

Darren lands a jab at Joseph's face. Blood spews from his nose. Two waiters from the restaurant arrive. One of them puts himself, arms spread, between Darren and Joseph.

"Stop or we'll call the police," the other one says.

More people arrive, including two men from security and the restaurant manager. Seeing that I'm bleeding, he calls for the medical staff and orders one of the waiters to get a napkin.

Darren is at my side, holding up my face to the moonlight. "Let me see."

I don't think I've lost any teeth. The blood is coming from my lip.

More guests from the wedding arrive, including Sharon and Cheryl. The waiter hands me a cloth napkin, which I hold against my lip. I panic for a second about the jewelry but the necklace and earrings are still on me.

A nurse arrives and exams me and Joseph,

while one of the security guards interviews bystanders about what happened.

"The son of a bitch broke my nose!" Joseph barks at the nurse, then glares over at Darren.

Darren balls his hand into a fist. "I'm not done with you."

"Yes, you are," says Sharon.

"You'll need to go to the local urgent care clinic to get a few stitches," the nurse says to me after assessing my lip.

After the nurse gives me and Joseph ice packs for our wounds, the security guards ask questions of the three of us. I reveal what happened between me and Joseph and can see Darren's color rising again. I'm asked if I want to press charges.

"If he doesn't press charges against Darren, then no," I answer.

The resort staff looks relieved.

"What do you mean you're not pressing charges?" Darren demands.

"I don't want anyone sitting in jail," I respond. "I'm sure that's not how Andrea and Preston want to end their wedding night."

Darren doesn't look satisfied.

"I agree," Sharon says. "Let it go. Let's just get Bridget to the clinic."

Darren grudgingly relents.

I look around for my shoe. Darren finds it and hands it to me. "Not a bad weapon."

The heel is broken, so Cheryl offers to fetch a new pair of shoes from our room. Sharon accompanies me and Darren to the clinic, where I get sewn up. I overhear Darren talking to JD on the phone.

"You know what'll happen if I see him again," Darren says.

"Don't worry. We got him set up at a different resort," JD replies.

"I have to apologize to the bride and groom," I say later as we head back to the resort.

"Why?" Darren asks, disgruntled. "Mok started it."

"It's still the polite thing to do. I hope they don't feel like we ruined their wedding reception."

Darren doesn't say anything. I get the feeling he's still brewing over what else he wants to do to Joseph.

"What matters is that you're okay right now," Sharon says.

Back at the villa, I change into one of the bathrobes and try to wash the stain from Elaine's drink out of the dress. After hanging it up, I examine my stitches in the mirror, running my finger over the unevenness of my lip.

"Don't pick at it," Darren says from the doorway.

"I wasn't," I object. "I've just never had stitches before. Broke my arm trying to skateboard, but no stitches."

Darren walks over, cups my jaw and looks over my stitches. "Guess this means I don't get to kiss you for a while."

I smile. "That's okay. There's plenty of other things you can do instead."

His eyes glimmer. "You got that right."

CHAPTER TWENTY-SIX

DARREN

Past

"You want to put a hit on Mok?" JD asks the following day.

Sitting on a lounge chair near the infinity pool with the midday sun glaring down at me, I entertain the idea for a second before replying, "Not worth it. If he had raped Bridge, then yes."

"How about a brutal beating?"

"It won't be satisfying unless I do it myself."

JD eyes a young woman in a skimpy bikini sitting at the swim-up bar.

"Where's Amy?" I ask.

"Still asleep."

The young woman smiles at JD, prompting him to say, "I'm gonna cool down in the water a bit."

After JD goes in, I decide to swim in the lap pool. I can't seem to settle my nerves. Every time I think about Mok, my blood pressure rises.

After several laps of IM, I feel a little better and return to my lounge chair and towel off.

My mother comes up to me. "How's Bridget?"

"She's working on some grant application, but she should be up here soon. She wants the chance to say goodbye."

My mother nods. "She's more interesting than I first thought. Still not the right girl for you, though. I'm surprised you're with a wonky type to begin with."

I put on my sunglasses and lie back. "Who says I need a 'right' girl? If I follow in Dad's footsteps, I'm better off with no one."

"You're right about that, especially since you can't keep her out of trouble even with people who *aren't* gangster. Joseph Mok is a nobody."

"He touched what belongs to me."

I think I spoke too emphatically, because my mother looks taken aback. I rub my temple. I know I'm the real reason Bridget has a split lip. If I hadn't gone after Mok, she wouldn't have stitches. I'm also fully aware I'm angry at myself, but I don't have any issues taking it out on Mok.

My mother continues, "You'd be better off *not* taking after your dad and being with a girl who's more *simple*."

"What do you mean by 'simple.' Bridget's not complicated."

My mother furrows her brow. "Yeah, but she

has her own goals. She's not just going to sit around supporting whatever you do all the time, especially if what you're doing involves more with the *Jing San*."

I recall how Bridget didn't stand around screaming like the other women. She jumped right into the fray. I smile. "No, she definitely didn't just sit around while I was trying to beat the shit out of Mok."

"She could have been hurt worse."

"You that worried about her?"

"I'm worried about *you*. What happens if you fall in love?"

I try to imagine what that would be like. I remember having a pretty bad crush on a girl in high school, then thinking I was in love with Jade Huang, who does bookkeeping for many triad members, but the emotions faded after a few months. That's about as close as I've come to being in love.

"You worry too much," I finally tell my mother.

"Do I? Maybe it's already happened?"

"What's already happened" I ask with exasperation.

"Maybe you've *already* fallen in love."

I don't respond. Women. They make such a big deal about everything. And I've done enough for my mother. I finished school for her. I stepped away from my father's legacy in the triad. So far.

There's no fucking way I'm giving up Bridget.

242

Not now. Maybe not ever.
    Shit.
    My mother might be right.

CHAPTER TWENTY-SEVEN

DARREN
Present

Despite the coolness of the basement, I feel warm. Very warm. Probably from the heat of my arousal combined with the heat of my anger as I stare down at Bridget. I kick aside any sympathy I feel seeing her with her legs forcefully folded by rope bondage, her arms bent with her wrists tied behind her neck and secured to a rope crotch, her face marked with my cum.

I can't believe I fell in love with this woman. That might be what I'm most angry about, and I'm pretty damn angry that she ran out on me.

My mother warned me about her. And she was right about Bridget. But stupid fucking me had to have her. I can't believe I was such a pathetic fool. Ready to turn my world upside down for her. Wanting to give her the best that I could. What a moron. What. A. Fucking. Moron.

"You like that?" I ask her, referring to the deep-throating, as I zip up my jeans. Not that she ever excelled at the skill, but she's definitely out of practice.

I smear some of the cum on her cheek down to her lips and push it in. "Taste good?"

"You know I love your cum," she says.

I snort. The old me would have believed that. I fist my hand into her hair and yank her head back. "Don't fucking patronize me."

"I—I missed it. I miss...us."

I can feel my anger boil. What "us?" She's the one who left.

Instead of pointing that out, I respond, "Yeah? You got anything else you want to tell me?"

"I miss you how good you made me come. I miss all the crazy shit you did to my body."

"Like what?"

"Like the sounding."

I remember how nervous she was her first time, but she liked it.

"What else?"

"The rope bondage, the anal plugs, the wax play."

"We did a lot, didn't we?"

She nods earnestly.

"It was fun, wasn't it?" I ask.

"Yes."

I grab her throat and snarl in her face,

"Bullshit."

If she liked it so much—if she really wanted to be with me—why did she leave?

She looks bewildered. "Why don't you believe me? You think I faked all those orgasms?"

"I believe I had you all wrong. I believed you were the good girl. But I guess the fact that you were into my kink and BDSM means you're actually a naughty girl. A very naughty girl."

Her eyes are large as she stares back at me. "I liked everything you did. I really did!"

Stop fucking lying to me!

In disgust, I step back from her and look away. I want to get my emotions under control. If I listen to her any longer, I might actually believe her. She sounds so fucking sincere. I might fall for her innocent tone.

I turn back to face her. "You said you liked everything I did?"

She nods.

"Well, you're in luck. I sent Marshall to pick up a few things. We'll see just how much you liked it all."

I walk over to where I left the suitcase, which I open to reveal some BDSM essentials: a flogger, wand, nipple and clit camps, ball gag, Ben Wa balls, dildo and lube.

"Remember all this fun stuff?"

She looks at them thoughtfully before nodding. "You introduced me to a lot, Darren."

For some reason, I don't like her speaking my name. She doesn't have the right to use my name.

Seeing my grim look and raised brows, she corrects herself. "Sir."

Picking up the hood she wore before, I put it back over her head. The deprivation of sight will keep her guessing in addition to enhancing her sense of touch.

I unwrap the bonds around her legs, then grab her by the arm and drag her over to the table. It's heavy and sturdy. I disengage the rope around her wrists from the crotch rope, pull her upper body over the table, and secure the end of the rope binding her wrists to a leg of the table. Her ass is positioned just off the table's edge. Next, I bind her ankles to opposite legs of the table before undoing the crotch rope.

I slip my hand between her thighs. She's still wet there, though probably somewhat sore or numb from the crotch rope. I give her rump a smack before returning to the suitcase. After selecting the ball gag, I walk over to the head of the table, pull her chin down and push the ball into her mouth. The fabric of the hood is trapped between her tongue and the ball, which will probably dry out her mouth. But why should I care about her comfort?

I go for the duotone Ben Wa balls, hollow with weights inside, and watch her body jump as I slide them along her slit and tease her clit before inserting them into her pussy. I spank her several times to get the balls to move. She groans. When I rub her between the legs, she moans even deeper. She's aroused. I can sense it.

From the suitcase, I get the flogger. Her body tenses, probably because she can hear me approaching. Unfurling the tails, I lash it across her ass. She grunts. I backhand the next strike, whipping the tips to her flesh for more sting. Bridget usually tolerates the flogger pretty easily, and I wish I had a paddle or cane instead, but the blows are enough to jar the balls inside of her. After several lashes, I check between her legs to find her wetness running down her inner thigh.

"Guess you're liking this," I remark.

My cock is hard again. I set the flogger back in the case and shed my pants. I can see the alertness in her body, wondering what's coming next. I push my cock at her pussy and sink into its delicious heat. This feels amazing. More amazing than I remember.

I start off with a few long, drawn strokes, relishing the sound of her muffled groans, before slamming into her. Each shove causes the table to move, so I grab her hips to keep her still, a wet, hot target for me to spear over and over.

I pull out and try out her other hole next. After slowly sinking balls deep into her ass, I start to thrust.

"Liking this, too, Bridge?" I ask, spanking her

with my pelvis as I piston in and out.

I fuck harder. She attempts to speak, but her words are incoherent beneath the hood and ball gag. It just sounds like whining and mumbling. And then screaming as her body trembles violently against the table. I feel her rectum spasm around my cock.

"You did not just come without my permission," I say.

My ardor is raging now. I pound myself into her. Her cries are no longer related to her orgasm, but I'm almost there. With blinding fury, my climax rings through me like a gong. My entire body tenses as I buck into her, unloading into her sweet, sweet ass. I allow myself to remain inside of her, her ass feeling tighter with every throb, until the hardness dissipates along with the quaking of my body.

I pull out of her and note some of my cum oozing down her crack. I walk over to the other side of the table to undo the end of the rope anchored to the leg. She doesn't move. Removing the hood and ball gag, I lift her jaw to meet her gaze and see that her eyes are glistening.

I don't like the conflict of emotions in me right now. I don't want to be feeling anything but righteous anger toward her. To support that, I ask, "What's the matter? I fuck you too hard, Bridge?"

Still breathing on the heavy side, she doesn't answer.

I replace the ball gag into the case, along with the hood. Standing behind her, I yank her up by her hair.

"You know you came without permission," I growl. "That means we'll have to add weights to the nipples clamps."

She looks nervous but doesn't protest.

"You think your nipples would be up for that?" I inquire as I run a finger over a nipple through her dress. She looks fuller than she did two years ago, especially in the chest. Her breasts look large on her, almost as if she got implants.

"You get augmentation surgery, Bridge?" I ask, reaching to grope a breast.

She shrugs away from me and looks down. "No. I just...put on some weight."

I grab her chin and make her look at me. "You're not lying to me, are you?"

"Why would I lie to you?"

"Yeah, why would you? 'Cause you have something to hide?"

"Something to hide...? Darren, I—I made a mistake. About us."

I cross my arms. "You did? Is that why you're on a date with Josh?"

"That was—my friends convinced me to— Wait, you know his name?"

It shouldn't matter one fuck who she goes on a date with. When I'm through with her, she can date a thousand guys. I'm done with her.

But first, I have to claim what's mine.

My son.

Excerpt
CLAIMED DARKER

CLAIMED

DARKER

EM BROWN

CHAPTER ONE

DARREN
Present

Hovering over her body, still tied face-down to the basement table, I don't have to see into her face to know that the wheels are turning in Bridget's head. I knew from day one she wasn't stupid. Even when she threw her drink in my face. One wouldn't expect that kind of action from the cerebral type—the type I don't usually involve myself with—but Bridget is...unexpected. Nuanced. Sometimes thoughtful, sometimes impulsive. A good girl out in the world but naughty as hell in the bedroom. I wonder if she's still like that, two years later.

Fuck it. It doesn't matter what she's like. I'm done with her. I'm sticking with simpler women. Women who don't overthink things, who don't challenge my scruples, and who don't dare to pull a disappearing act on me.

But before I leave her to her fate, I'm going to

make the most of what's mine. I'm going to use her body till she can't move a limb. I'm going to blow past her limits, even the hard ones, because limits—and safe words—are built on respect and trust. And she broke both those when she skipped town with my son.

CHAPTER TWO

BRIDGET
Past

The morning of my flight back to California, as I examine myself in the bathroom mirror, I ask myself: was Phuket worth getting stitches in my lip?

Yes, oh yes. Without a doubt.

Not only did I get to experience one of the most beautiful places on earth—my first time out of the U.S. and I got to go to Thailand—I got to spend time with Darren. And he seems to have been extra sweet ever since I got my busted lip, thanks to my attempt to intervene in a fight between him and Joseph Mok, an old rival. As if he thinks I'm maimed, Darren hasn't been as hard or rough the times we've had sex. He hasn't thrown in any BDSM elements, which I'm surprised I kind of miss. I guess I like the way Darren keeps me on my toes.

Last night he surprised me with a romantic dinner on the beach. The resort staff had set up oversized pillows and a table just for two beneath a canopy of tulle and organza.

"How can I thank you enough for this trip?" I had asked him part way through dinner. "Everything has been amazing, from the flight to the accommodations to the clothes."

"You'll be thanking me," he had replied with a glimmer in his eyes. "A night at my club, remember?"

I hadn't forgotten. It's pretty hard to rid my mind of the image of clothespins being ripped off a woman's naked body, one of the first scenes I had seen after accidentally wandering into the BDSM side of the club Darren owns. What would he want to do to me? I weathered the spanking he gave me with my hairbrush. The anal plug was awkward but surprisingly erotic. But I know he's going to up the game at his club, and now I feel beholden to endure as much as possible. Not because Darren said I had to but because it's human nature to want to return a favor.

"I probably owe you more than just one night," I had joked to see what his response would be. It wasn't my choice to fly in a suite, stay in a beach cabin at a luxury resort, or have his manager buy designer clothes for me. But I had enjoyed it, nonetheless, so it was time to pay the piper.

"The agreement going into this was one night," he had said, "but if you're offering more, I won't refuse."

"Let's see how the first night goes," I had replied.

I had expected him to reassure me then that he'd go gentle on me or that we'd take it slow, but he didn't do any of that.

"This is the part where you tell me I have nothing to worry about," I had prodded.

"I can't predict what you will or won't worry about," he had replied placidly.

That didn't help put me at ease.

"I'll have a safe word, right?" I had asked.

"'Course."

That had made me feel better. A little.

I finger the stitches on my bottom lip. Supposedly the stitches will just dissolve when my lip heals. I haven't told Aunt Coretta, the woman who spent a good many years helping my grandmother raise me, about my split lip. I had forgotten to call her the night of the wedding and subsequent brawl, and she had been a little worried. Flying half way round the world with a man I didn't know all that well wasn't the most prudent thing to do. It was something my mom would do. And I didn't want to be like my mom, who basically abandoned me with my grandmother so she could gallivant around Europe with rich or pseudo-rich men. I don't know for sure how she ended up with my father, who served in the military and was far from rich, except that she was on the rebound.

"Leave your stitches alone."

I turn to see Darren standing at the bathroom

entrance with his arms crossed in front of him.

"They feel weird," I reply, glancing back into the mirror.

He walks over to me and grasps my chin, forcing me to meet his gaze. "Touch them again, and your ass will pay for it."

My backside tingles. "Okay, okay. What's the big deal anyway?"

"You never had stitches before?"

I shake my head.

"I have," he says, releasing me. "Twice. The first time, I picked at them and ended up reopening the wound."

"Why'd you need stitches?"

"I was twelve. JD dared me to leap over the stairs in front of our school on my bike. I crashed and hit my chin."

"And the second time?"

He pauses before replying, "Another accident. Teen boys are prone to that."

"What happened?"

He turns away dismissively. "It was stupid shit."

"What kind of stupid shit?"

He doesn't respond right away.

"I can imagine some pretty stupid shit," I offer.

He looks a little exasperated but says, "I accidentally shot myself with a gun."

My eyes widen. "What were you doing with a gun?"

"It wasn't mine. It belonged to my bodyguard."

"You had a bodyguard?"

"My father was paranoid that year. But my mom had the bodyguard fired after what happened."

I'm curious to know what prompted his father's paranoia, but that might be a sensitive subject, so I ask, "Were you hurt badly?"

"Bullet went into my leg."

"How did that happen?"

"The safety wasn't on the gun. I was fooling around, the gun fell to the ground and went off."

I gasp. "You were lucky the bullet didn't land anyplace worse."

H grins. "There was a moment when my mom lit into me that I wish the bullet *had* hit me in a worse place."

"I can see that about your mom. She's a tough lady. I like her."

I'm not entirely sure Sharon Lee returns the sentiment, however. She was nice to me after the brawl and accompanied me and Darren to the clinic where I got my stitches, but I've caught her looking at me oddly a few times, like I'm some strange zoo creature.

"You ready?" Darren asks me. "Our bags are in the car already."

"'Our' bags?" I echo. "Aren't you staying an extra week?"

"Why would I want to? Mok left, so I can't break his nose a second time."

I grab my purse and we walk out of the cabin.

"You were able to change your flight?"

"It was easy."

"Well, we'll be flying in separate parts of the plane. I had Cheryl downgrade my flight to economy."

"You think my manager wouldn't have told me that?"

"Hope you like it in coach then."

"Hope *you* like it in the suite."

I stop. "You changed my flight?"

"I'm not flying economy, especially on an international flight."

"Okay, but I'd feel better flying coach."

He shakes his head at me. "You are one weird-ass chic, Bridge."

"The more you do stuff like this, the more I feel I owe you."

His eyes taken on a darker, molten quality. "Maybe that's the idea."

I don't have a response.

Amy, my friend and roommate from Cal, comes up to us. "I wish you'd stay longer."

"I wish I could, too," I answer. "But I can't miss much more school and work."

I wonder that Amy can seem so nonchalant about her classes and job. I know she's missing at least one test in her chem class, though she's so cute, she can probably talk her professor into letting her take it when she wants.

"Where's JD?" I inquire.

"On a business call," Amy says. "He's pretty mad. Something work-related. Like a bad shipment or something. It sounds super serious. I'm actually worried about him."

She looks over to Darren, who puts on his sunglasses even though we're standing in the shade of several sugar palm trees.

"He'll be fine," Darren says.

"Does this kind of thing happen often?" Amy asks.

Darren shrugs. "Things have always worked out for my cousin."

Amy appears a little more at ease. "I didn't realize his line of business could be so stressful."

Darren doesn't say anything further on the topic. I remember that JD imports and exports chemical compounds or something like that.

"I'll go check out," Darren says before heading over to the reception.

Once he's out of earshot, Amy gushes, "Can you believe how lucky the two of us have been? Spending a week in paradise with two super hot guys? It feels like I'm dreaming, and I hope I never wake up!"

I finger the stitches in my lip.

"Except for you getting hurt, of course," Amy adds.

"Still worth it," I reply.

"It's too bad that Mok guy didn't end up in jail."

I agree, but Darren threw the first punch

between the two of them, so if Mok went, Darren might have as well. And apparently both men have sat in jail before. Which didn't surprise me terribly when Darren had told me. I've always sensed there was an edge to Darren, and I don't usually go for guys like that. If it weren't for the chemistry...which I don't understand either. Pheromones, I guess?

"The only thing that would make this trip perfect," Amy continues, "is if JD weren't so stressed about work and if *she* wasn't here."

I follow her gaze to the swim-up bar in the pool where a beautiful young woman wearing a glittering gold one-piece swimsuit that has less fabric to it than a bikini sits. I wish I could reassure her that she has nothing to worry about, but I just don't know Darren's cousin well enough. I've caught JD glancing at other women with appreciation in his eyes, which doesn't automatically make him a player or disqualify him for relationship material, but I still get a less than trustworthy sense. I should probably apply that sentiment to Darren, even though he seems to have rebuffed the women who have come onto him during our stay here in Phuket. Noting that Darren's most recent ex-girlfriend is a lingerie model, I think it's probably a matter of time before he does give in to the attentions of women hotter than me.

Well, it would have been fun while it lasted. Frankly, as much as I'm attracted to him, I'm not sure that Darren's relationship material either. At least not for me.

CHAPTER THREE

DARREN
Present

I release her hair and her head falls back toward the table I tied her to. Stepping back, I survey her body stretched across the surface, her dress bunched at the hips, exposing her ass. It's a little more supple than I remember it, but it felt as good as before. Tight, too. So maybe she was telling the truth when she said she hadn't let anyone back there since she left me about two years ago.

"Wh-Where's Josh right now?" she asks.

I had let slip the name of the guy back in Denver whom I had paid off to secure a date with her. After Josh had cut short their date, claiming his grandfather was ill, one of my men, pretending to be a cab driver, was waiting for Bridget when she walked out of the restaurant.

"You think I give a fuck?" I reply. "What's the matter? You worried about your boyfriend?"

Jealousy roars through me. It feels like she

cheated on me, even though we aren't together. I know a guy who used to run extortion for the *Jing San Triad* and who shot his girlfriend for cheating on him. The basement we currently occupy is a good place to kill someone. 'Old Dog,' a hired hitman in the triad, owns the house and told me he tortured a triad traitor for days in this basement. There's a drain in the floor, and a hose that can attach to the cement sink in the corner. Ideal for washing away the evidence.

But I'm not that cold-blooded, though I wish I were right now. When I'm through with Bridget, she's going to wish she never crossed me.

"He's not my boyfriend," she denies. "He's just some guy I met at a cafe."

Her protestations only make me more angry. Moments ago she had claimed to miss 'us.' Which was bullshit. If that was true, she wouldn't have left. She wouldn't have not told me that I had a son.

"Yeah?" I ask as I survey the basement for something I can work with. Earlier, I had her wrists tied to the exposed pipes above. It must have killed her feet to have to stand in the heels she's wearing. I remember how she hated wearing high heels, which she deemed misogynistic. So it's her own damn fault for wearing them now.

She turns her head to look at me. "I wasn't that interested."

"Not interested? That's why you got all dressed

up for him, why you're wearing lacy panties." I walk over to where her ass rounds the edge of the table and sink my fingers into a lush sphere. "How far were you planning to go with him?"

"I wasn't!"

"Don't fucking lie to me, Bridge."

"I'm not!"

I shake her ass to rattle the Ben Wa balls still in her pussy before slapping a cheek. "Lying is going to get you a serious punishment."

"What about what you're doing? Kidnapping and…"

"And what?"

She hesitates before spitting out, "And sexual torment."

"Torment?" I echo. "I thought you missed this. You said you missed all the crazy shit I did to your body. Or was that a fucking lie?"

She lowers her gaze. "It wasn't."

"And you came just now. With my cock buried in your ass." I slide my hand between her thighs. The wetness there makes my head spin. "Didn't you?"

"Yes, sir."

"You're just racking up the punishments."

Even though her arms are stretched in front of her because her wrists are secured to a leg of the table, her shoulders seem to sag.

"I forgot our rules. I'm sorry, sir."

Sorry doesn't cut it anymore.

I saunter over to a suitcase I had Marshall bring

down to me. I review the BDSM paraphernalia inside and ask, "So what punishment do you want to start with?"

Printed in Great Britain
by Amazon

68427039R00159